Attorney Gone

DIANE SMITH

ATTORNEY GONE

iUniverse books may be ordered through booksellers or by contacting:

iUniverse
1663 Liberty Drive
Bloomington, IN 47403
www.iuniverse.com
844-349-9409

Because of the dynamic nature of the Internet, any web addresses or links contained in this book may have changed since publication and may no longer be valid. The views expressed in this work are solely those of the author and do not necessarily reflect the views of the publisher, and the publisher hereby disclaims any responsibility for them.

Any people depicted in stock imagery provided by Getty Images are models, and such images are being used for illustrative purposes only. Certain stock imagery © Getty Images.

ISBN: 978-1-6632-4291-4 (sc)
ISBN: 978-1-6632-4292-1 (e)

Print information available on the last page.

iUniverse rev. date: 07/20/2022

*A*bigail Herrera was in the kitchen when her son came in. She had just made lunch for her and her small daughter and she was cleaning up when her 18 year old son walked into the back door.

"Why are you here Michael?" She asked the useless son-of-a-bitch. She tried to be patient, she really did, but the little bastard was a mess. This would be the third job that her husband had gotten for their son, and now here he was, standing in the middle of the kitchen, acting like nothing was wrong, and as if he was completely innocent.

Michael walked over to his mother who was standing at the sink rinsing dishes and put his arm around her rather plumb soft body.

"If I were you, Michael, and I didn't want my face slapped, very hard I might add, I'd scoot my ass over to the table and I'd sit it down and tell me why you aren't at work."

"Geez Man!" The kid said, letting her go quickly and stomping over to the table. "What the hell, Ma! What kind of mother slaps their full grown son, I wonder. It just ain't natural." He exploded, throwing his chunky Mexican body into the old yellow kitchen chair. Now he was really scared, but it didn't matter; he needed her help.

"Get yourself a cup of coffee and start talking now."

"Oh come on Ma, you know that I don't drink that vile shit."

"Well I do. Get me a cup and starting talking, Michael." She said as she wiped down the spotless but wet counter.

He got the coffee and sat it on the table at the other end.

Abigail sat down and waited.

"Well, see Ma, there's this girl."

"And she's pregnant."

"Aw come on, Ma! No she ain't pregnant. That was last year." He lied.

"Last year? So why are you telling me this. Michael?"

"Well, because, well because…."

"Spit it out now; I will give you 2 minutes of my undivided attention. You of all people know that I don't have time for any of this right now; you know that this is the day I go grocery shopping, so if you have something to tell me, just do it. If you can't find the words, there's a skillet sitting right there on the stove; maybe if I smack you in the head with it, you will be able to remember why exactly you aren't at work but have decided to come home instead, Michael." She said, having lost all patience with her oldest son.

He looked over at the skillet, contemplating his next words. He knew his mother wouldn't actually beat him, so he certainly didn't worry about that.

"Are you hungry?"

"Yeah, Ma. I'm real hungry."

"I can make you lunch and you can tell me why you're here. Talk, Michael, but make it quick; your 2 minutes start now."

"So anyway, there was this real young little girl in the park all by herself. She was there all day just sitting and watching us play football. I knew she was hungry and she looked kind a scared too, so when the game was over, I went and sat down next to her, you know to try to help if I could."

Yeah, right, she thought but said nothing as she made him a baloney and mayonnaise sandwich, the idiot's favorite. No wonder he didn't have a brain in his head, it had all turned to baloney mixed with the chemicals they used to process this shit, she thought.

"So anyway, she didn't have nowhere to go. It was getting dark and everyone was gone home. Gang members liked the park and it was getting real dark. So I had to protect her because she was so little and all. And then I took her to the cabin." He said quickly.

"The cabin? Our cabin?"

"Yeah."

"Why didn't you bring her here Michael?"

She knew goddamned good and well why the horny little Mexican weasel hadn't brought her here.

"It just didn't feel like a real good idea, Ma."

"I'll bet."

"Now what does that mean?" Putting on his usual act of total innocence.

"How old is this child you're so happy to protect?"

"I don't know."

"Does she have breasts?"

"Well of course she got breasts. She's full-blooded Mexican."

"Okay. So bring her here."

"Well, that's the thing. I went up there this weekend and the girl had a baby."

Okay, here it was. "And who's the father of this baby??"

"Don't ask me. I ain't never touched her." He lied like the bold faced trooper he had become.

"It's freezing Michael. It's almost Christmas, for God's sake and the cabin doesn't have heat!!"

"Yeah but she ain't cold and she's got plenty to eat, I made real sure of that one."

Abigail Maria Herrera stood up and made the sign of the cross and then untied her apron. "Let's go."

He stood up and they went to the boy's old beat up car. Thank sweet Mother Mary the protector of children because of her son and all, he thought as he headed toward the very forested very cold cabin hidden in the woods.

Abbey went into the bedroom and looked at the tiny face, brushing her hair out of face and sat down on the edge of the bed.

"Are you okay?"

"Yes Ma'am." The little girl said, a newborn suckling on her full breast.

Abbey took the baby and found a clean towel and wrapped the tiny, tiny girl with the wild thick black hair; just like Michael's she thought, but she wasn't angry; she was thrilled to be her holding her first grandchild in her arms. She took the baby to her son and went back to the girl to help her dress, and they went home. She made arrangements for them to be married in the little Catholic chapel and they had a wonderful reception.

Michael got a new job, and this time he stayed, becoming quite good at any and every construction project they could throw his way, a natural talent his father always said proudly. With time, he went to school to become a contractor and opened his own business. He was extremely successful and he bought his sweet mama a lovely house on the edge of town. Dad helped him run the company like a well-oiled machine and they prospered. He was so damned proud of his used to be stupid and quite useless little boy.

And that was how Danielle came into the world. The fiery Mexican bitch was now bossing him around like he was a fucking half-wit. He had fired her countless times but she would just ignore him of course. He owed her money and she wasn't leaving until the fucker paid up she would say. She had Luke's check book of course, and she was writing checks left and right for herself, stealing him blind he knew. Fucking bitch. He'd get her with time, of course, and he'd make damned certain that they threw the book at the thieving broad. He was a lawyer and a damned good one. To make matters even worse was that she would never let him touch her and he was quite sick of the stupid Mexican maiden, always acting like the Virgin Mary incarnate. She had absolutely no respect. But she knew the law and he knew he could never be as successful as he was without her. Too bad she was such a cunt, he often told her, but as usual, she just ignored her boss and wrote more checks, stealing him blind, Goddamnit!

Luke McNally was an attorney and a damned good one if you asked him. He knew his way around the courthouse and every prison in the state of South Carolina and Georgia. He had been raised in Savannah and was a quite well known attorney. Everyone wanted Luke McNally. They knew he'd either get the jury to find his unfortunate client innocent or help the client to cut a deal with the district attorney's office. No matter how heinous the crime, if the district attorney didn't have absolute evidence or an outright confession from the victim, an unfortunate situation that Luke would simply blame on the duress and outright abuse of his client, and they many times walked out of court a free man. But that certainly didn't happen very often unless the client was a first time offender. Hardened criminals knew their rights and would never consider talking to the authorities without an attorney present. Of course, some criminal acts were so heinous that life in prison was unavoidable; but that was life. The world was better off without the fucking idiots anyway. Most of them deserved to hang to his way of thinking, but duty called, and so did his reputation as a criminal lawyer, so he did his best to get the animals back on the street. They would very likely all be returning clients again until there was no way left to save them and off they'd go where they should have been from the beginning, but not before he soaked them for as much drug selling money as he could get, of course. They weren't going to need it where they were going anyway.

Luke McNally loved women, any woman. There was always something there to like as far as he was concerned. He was 30 years old and had never married. Way too boring for him; he just couldn't imagine why any man in his right mind would want to be chained to a bitch who bossed him around and spent his money and twisted a man's balls until they turned blue, making it impossible for him to think for himself any longer. No sireee; that just wasn't for him. Not now, not ever....well....maybe someday when he was starting to get old and couldn't get it up anymore, then maybe.

Luke McNally had more money than he knew what to do with. He never left town and he could never think of anything to buy anymore, so it piled up silently in his savings account as each case was either won or lost, or at least it tried to pile up, he said with total disgust to the fucking Mexican slut sitting at the front desk, always acting like she was actually earning all that money that she would steal every Friday. He had no idea what the sum was; he just didn't care actually. It wasn't the sum total, but the principle of the fucking thing; but there was nothing he could do about it right now anyway. Far too busy trying to win court cases.

But Danielle knew. She robbed him on a regular basis, always telling him to just shut the fuck up, and then she would have the audacity to call him a cheap bastard. But again, nothing he could do about it right now. He had to get to court. With time, he would retire and travel the world. He'd work just one more year and then hit the skies or the seas or the road. Didn't matter which way he went. He was just too busy to give that much of a thought right now. What would the stupid bitch do then he often wondered, and he fantasized every now and then about how much she would miss him when he disappeared and left her thieving ass to fend for herself. The bitch would starve to death he thought with great satisfaction, but for now, he had to get to court.

He sat at his one beautiful possession. The large, gleaming walnut desk was his absolute pride and joy as it glistened below him in the dark office, lit by two small lamps in each corner of the desk. The lamps were never turned off. Many times he slept in his office on the big leather couch, but this morning a family sat there. One mother, one daughter, and one son. He listened and they talked. He never took notes because he had his trusty recorder and then the lovely, long-legged receptionist would come into the office and take the tape from the recorder and get busy typing the voices word for word. He would come out of his office sometimes and drag her off to lunch down the street. They were things to talk about and he would give her her instructions as they ate.

She was sharp as a fucking tack, many times sitting with him in court, taking notes and looking up case after case to show him a clear-cut case that would help with an objection for his client. Man, this young girl was priceless, he would admit then and only then; the admission soon to be forgotten as he got busy with the next client. Who knew? Luke had hired her because of her creamy skin glistening with youth, and her long thick black hair. Her breasts were oversized for her little frame and her slender legs seemed to actually be getting longer. At the time of her hiring, he had no idea that he wouldn't be able to run his office without her. He just wanted to have sex with the very young and lovely long haired wench. He had planned to get what he wanted from her and then eventually let her go as soon as he tired of her so that he could get someone in there who actually knew what they were doing. He really didn't have time to train the young lady, and he sure as hell wasn't interested in training the sweet young thing anyway. At least not in office stuff anyway.

It was once again a crazy busy morning, Danielle thought as she made what felt like reams of copies, one for the court, and one for the file, which she would file along with the hundreds of other neatly alphabetized folders on the shelves that ran along the wall behind her desk. Right now she was just finishing up a client who had come in yesterday. She thought it was a waste of time, but it was her job, and there were repeat offenders of course, which certainly shortened her work. This particular criminal was a fucking drug lord and a cop killer and he sure as hell wouldn't be living outside of prison for very much longer anyway. He was caught red handed and there was no way out for the loser idiot now. Just a bunch of damned work for her. Too many innocent and not so innocent people had died because of him, sometimes families with small children. It didn't matter a goddamned second to him. His victim, just a kid, should have obeyed him, he told them. He was a thief and he couldn't let him get by with it or everyone would be stealing his money. He had a business to run after all. He had escaped to Mexico many times to avoid justice, always sneaking back into the country to wait for a new shipment of cocaine or meth or PCP for him to sell in the streets after it was cut or separated and distributed to his young dealers that he ruled with an iron fist.

The Mexican cartel knew exactly what to do, seldom getting caught at the border anymore. But when they did, they simply accepted the loss and had the next shipment carried by 100s of willing peasants over the border and onto waiting U-Haul rentals to drive to Miami or Chicago or New York City because the Mexican drug lords needed to lay low until they could figure out who, if anyone, had ratted on them; then they would either pay that person more money and put them on the payroll and make that person their friend for a little while; but what usually happened was that they would kill that person, shoot them assassination style right where they happened to be that day. No one cared. It didn't matter to them where the drugs ended up. The money was never ending, millions of dollars for the US drug lords like Jose Manuela, and the new Cartels that moved in had always been treated like kings on the streets of every major city, mostly because they were vicious and no one wanted to be their targets if they could help it.

Marvin Johnson, the young man sitting on the couch this morning was the son of a sweet old man who had been violently murdered. He had done nothing, but he evidently got in someone's way. He told Luke McNally of the death of his sweet father. He had been there and watched the whole thing, hiding in the corner of the dark garage as the men beat him and then cut his throat, dragging him to the nearest tree and stringing his dead body up high to swing in the wind. He hadn't been able to help his father, all he could do was hide in the dark, but he knew the men and he wanted justice. No one would listen to him, simply taking notes and promising the impossible. This young man was much damaged from the horrific experience he had sustained as he had watched the vicious slaughter of his beloved father, Luke thought. Who in the hell wouldn't be after what he had been forced to watch. It had been brutal and twice as horrible when it was someone you loved. If they had seen him or found his hiding place, the boy would not be sitting here today, that was for sure. Whoever they were, and McNally was pretty certain he knew who was behind this, these people left no witnesses, not ever.

But now, sitting in his office, the mother and daughter listened, Colleen crying softly, her head down as her absolutely gorgeous young daughter held her hand. She had been away at school that morning, returning to cops and yellow tape across the yard. Valerie said nothing, listening quietly to her brother. She would be no help thought Luke. He thought about the girl but decided against trying to seduce her. He could tell that she was definitely interested but as far as he was concerned, there was nothing worse than a sad woman who was prone to depression and tears. He preferred the happy hookers who were full of sexual energy and without a care in the world, thank you.

When they left, Danielle came to his office and took the tape out of the recorder, having to lean over Luke who was not going to move out of her way. Okay, she thought, here it comes. Horny bastard; when was he ever going to give up the battle? He moved his chair back and grabbed her, pulling her into his arms and moving her thick black hair over one shoulder so that he could suck on her neck. Danielle had learned to just accept the assaults. The money was good and she loved the manly things he did anyway. If her big tough Mexican brother knew what was going on, he would very likely beat his sister for being a whore she told him, and then he'd slash Luke's fat neck just for fun. But of course she didn't have a brother, and even though Luke didn't know that, he seemed to be completely unconcerned of the danger she warned him of.

This man wasn't going to ruin her career in this office or any other place. He had plenty of women that he called in the evenings to play with, just not her, that was damned sure. She had no intentions of allowing a man of McNally's caliber anywhere near her. She wanted someone with substance, someone she would be able to trust at all times, a best friend to take the journey through life with, if such a creature even existed, which was highly unlikely as far as she could tell. His sexual exploits were nothing to be ashamed of he'd assure her happily. Many of his women were from the escort service, and some of them were gorgeous black hookers he would tell her. He was responsible for contributing money into the economy to make the world a better place...or so he said. What fun she would think as she closed up for the night and went home.

The next drug dealing prick came to the office and this one was a doozy, she thought. He wouldn't answer any questions; he didn't even look at McNally as he coaxed him to tell his story, but he did stare at the lovely long-haired beauty sitting right there in front of him, thanks to her asshole boss. He knew the charges against him would be dropped, and what he wanted right now, this minute was sex. Danielle ignored him as she waited, getting more and more irritated by the minute. McNally didn't need her of course but he needed the attention she brought to certain half-wits and this Mexican trash was about as stupid as they came; however, his ridiculous reputation was at stake here, you know what I mean, Danielle? No I don't, and I really could care less, you half-wit loser, she always retorted with disgust.

"I wan-chew to be my woman."

"And you can certainly have her; blow jobs are part of the job description, but right now we have work to do if you want to stay out of jail, Manuel."

His proclamation didn't faze Danielle one bit…she had heard it all before from this asshole.

But he wasn't listening. He stood up and moved to her chair, and he unzipped and pulled the ridiculously long snake through the zipper.

"I got this for you, Baby." It was hard and it stood straight out at attention, level with her face, unfortunately. He grabbed her face and tried to shove it in her mouth. She turned her head away but he was determined to get his penis in her mouth. She shoved him hard, but he went backwards only a little ways and then came back to stand above her. She didn't even bother to look to her asshole boss for any kind of help. She had been through this before. Just part of the job the idiot would say.

McNally sat there, his feet up on his desk, puffing on a cigar with his outrageously big hands clasped behind his head as he watched the drama unfold before him, grinning like a fucking Cheshire cat as he watched. He'd get up in a minute and help him get her clothes off if necessary. He swore once again that this was now going to be a major role in her job description from here on out. He had certainly paid more than his fair share to make her do this one thing for him. She was his employee after all and he paid her very, very well; better than he knew, actually. It was her job after all to do as he, the boss, instructed, and he tired of her endless virgin pretentions. Today was definitely the day, he had assured the skinny, lanky trash he had agreed to defend for an outrageous sum of money, just for fun, he told him, to spice up his day a little.

McNally watched with a lighthearted interest, totally unconcerned that she was about to be assaulted, but that was okay she thought. Did the stupid idiot never learn? He would pay dearly for this because he watched the whole scene that was unfolding in front of him with humor, simply enjoying the show, and never once made a move to protect his employee. She stood up in front of the skinny boy who thought he was a big man, but he didn't move. He pushed her back into the chair and she stood up immediately again and lifted her long slender leg and kneed him right square in the nuts. He went down slowly to the floor, but he didn't cry out. She stepped around him and headed back to the office.

"I'm warning you Danielle, stay out of my money. Every time things don't go your way you use it as an excuse to steal from me!" He yelled from his desk. "Don't think I'm not on to you because that would be a big mistake lady. Jail might not be that much fun, if you know what I mean!" He shouted at the small teen's back.

She ignored him and went out the front door and walked in the small parking lot. She flipped her phone open and called the bank. She had $15,000 transferred to her very, very healthy savings account. She was rolling in money now and she intended to finally spend it. She walked around her rusted out Honda. It was on its last leg and she refused to spend one more dime on this piece of shit. She would go on Saturday and buy a new one, a little convertible sports car; a BMW that she had seen at the dealership; it was just perfect for her and she intended to have it. She had seen it last weekend and the cute salesman promised to hold it for her. It was exactly the color she wanted too. If McNally insisted on using her to excite his lousy clients, then he was certainly going to pay and he was going to pay out the nose.

The next poor, innocent victim came in an hour later. There was absolutely no proof that he had killed anyone or had even ordered the hit. He too was more interested in the Mexican beauty in the other room, asking Luke questions about his receptionist.

"You fucking her, lawyer man?" He asked his black, hard-as-marble eyes staring at the Mexican princess, but at least he kept his hands to himself like a good Italiano who had more than enough women to keep him busy anyway.

"Sometimes." He lied. "But there's a lot to do around here and I don't always have time for her."

"She your girl?"

"Fuck no. I don't take hostages. Too much pussy out there." He said matter-of-factly as he smoked his cigar and they looked out at Danielle.

She was at her desk listening to the exchange with disgust.

"Dream on, you lying son-of-a-bitch." She shouted as she stuck the tape in the machine to start the transcription on the half-wit who had tried his best to assault her; it needed to be finished for court tomorrow, and she was hoping the little asshole would have the book thrown at him. It was time to get the little monster off the streets once and for all.

When she felt their stare, knowing that they were still discussing her, she got up and went to the copy machine out of sight of the office door and the stupid bastards in the other room. But, it never failed. Luke would come to the door and tell her bring a pad and pencil. He always made her sit directly across from the horny client. He needed information and he needed it now if he was going to win the case. The perfect solution was right here. She never had a choice. She'd go into the office and join them, quite reluctantly but always taking a seat with her pad and pencil, far too aware of what was coming. She was getting so sick of his shit, she always told the who-gives-a-shit-it's-your-job boss who completely ignored the ranting and oh-so irritating little virgin; this had gone on long enough and the woman needed a good fuck, he told her constantly. Then she'd go back to her transcription, and would toss the stupid, time-wasting notes she had scribbled on her pad into the trash. Just another fun day at the office.

The innocent murdering drug prick was finally leaving, thank the good Lord in the heavens. But no. Luke stood above her and told her that the authorities would be there in less than 15 minutes to arrest this poor innocent young man and he had to beat them to the judge so he could set bail for this poor fucking half-wit victim.

"Come on Danielle, I need you there."

"Keep your hands off me McNally or your balls will be the next in line to suffer."

He reached down and took her impossibly skinny arm and dragged her out of the chair and the Italian druggie watched and grinned.

"If you want this tape finished today, you will go away and let me do my work, Luke. I don't think that's asking too much." She said trying to reason with him.

"Sorry, no can do. You can't be trusted. I know you'll tell them where we are the minute they step through this door. You always do that, lady, and now you must suffer the consequences of your endless indiscretions against me, your boss, I might add."

He dragged her to his car and tossed her in the back seat, but she didn't bother to try to get out; he had the child locks punched on all three doors, leaving only his free to open.

They were there for all of 20 minutes and she turned and walked out of the courtroom. She would call a cab. It was Friday and she had to find a lovely, lovely convertible BMW sports car, almost $100,000, but the office would pay the monthly payments anyway. Why in the hell had she waited for so long?

She thought about quitting, but there was always too much work. However, she swore that she was going to very soon. She had many friends in the courthouse and the district attorney's office, and they all agreed that it was time for her to hit the road and finally make some decent money, because, of course, they had no way of knowing how much money she really made. However, she did want a bigger apartment and better clothes, so money was certainly the issue here, and she was quite certain that she wouldn't be leaving this place where her fortunes flowed anytime soon, and besides that, Luke McNally was one interesting and fun man to work for and she just didn't want to leave the idiot.

That night as she drank and smoked, someone broke into Luke McNally's office. Her files were pulled from the shelves and tossed on the floor when she got to work. Thank God she had just recently filled boxes with old cases and had taken them to storage or she'd be going through files and sorting for months.

She had no idea what they were looking for, maybe something she had already archived because as far as she could tell, nothing was missing. Luke never did come to work that day, so she locked up and drove her beat up car to her aunt's house. She and her young cousin finally went shopping and she bought her clothes, lots of clothes. School was starting soon and she wanted the lovely teenager to wear the best. She had thought many times of enrolling in school and she did just that during her lunch hour on Monday. She had put it off long enough now. She'd have to start with her Associates, but she looked forward to the challenge.

At the advice of the counselor she had talked to at the university, she registered on line and started classes that same evening. She had the option to test out and she began to study day and night, taking the books to work. Luke never noticed as long as she got the work done. She had her Associates in less than six months because she tested out early on many of the classes, studying every minute until she was confident that she would pass with flying colors. She intended to enroll in a Master's degree program, but changed her mind at the last minute and enrolled in law school. The LSAT was a breeze for her and she passed with flying colors. She was accepted into law school which was to begin within the next month. It was easy for her because she knew all there was to know about the law. She hated getting up in front of her class, but with time, she shone. In three years she completed her law degree. It was easy. She always had the right answers and the perfect tests. Then she graduated on a cold Saturday afternoon as her aunt and her little cousin sat in the audience. She was now officially an attorney at law, but who cared? Certainly not the 100s of other attorneys in this town; everyone was struggling to make a name for themselves but were forced to join law firms and wait their turns or try it on their own if they had the resources or go to work for the District Attorney's office.

The now 21 year old didn't say a word to Luke. She had been with this man for 6 long years and it was certainly time to move on. She'd been hired when she was just 15, lying of course about her age; but he certainly wouldn't have cared about that, he just wanted her young body, as he had told her so many times. He was 26 at the time and he needed it pretty much every day he would tell her, or he was 29 and then 32 with the same old story, like a broken record that never shut up about his manly needs. He instinctively knew that this shy little waif was a virgin and he wasn't about to pass this up. He was tired of the endless parade of young hookers he hired from the escort service; plus they were damned expensive and he was tired of giving them his money. He wanted something that smelled fresh, like a little innocent girl just starting her journey into the world of womanhood. Yessiree; he was the best teacher she could ever have he would tell her over and over again. At first she was shocked and even terrified that he might force her against her will and he said shocking things to the young teen, but as time went on, she realized the idiot was hardly a threat.

She'd open her law office next summer but that took money and lots of it. Then she'd go to the desk and write herself a very healthy check for cash and deposit it in her savings on the way home. Luke never once looked at the check book, simply bitching about the money she was extorting from him, but he really had no proof of that and he didn't seem that interested in his accounts anyway. She had figured out a long time ago that all McNally needed to make himself a happy man was enough money to eat well and to pay for his hookers.

One night after a particularly busy day, she had gone to bed early, watching an old and very boring movie that lulled her into slumber. She woke to a man standing above her bed, but for some reason, she was not the least bit frightened. She could tell that he had no intention of attacking as he turned and sat in the chair across from the bed, obviously waiting for her to wake up fully. At first, she thought it was Luke who had broken into the apartment, looking for the money she owed him...or some such shit. She didn't scream, she doubted anyone would hear her at this hour anyway. She got out of bed and got dressed as ordered and then she was led out to a Mercedes parked at the curb. It was 2:00 a.m. her watch said. She had remembered her cigarettes thank God. She was going to need them before the night was over she thought.

She was taken to a beautiful penthouse where an older very distinguished gentleman waited. The man escorted her into the room, and he was excused to go home to Maria and his children by the kind gentleman. He asked her if she would like something to drink and she told him that wine would be wonderful. Since he was smoking a cigar, she pulled her cigarettes and asked if he would mind, which of course he agreed, bringing her a crystal ashtray for her from the bar. As she drank her wine calmly, she waited for him to tell her why she was there, but he seemed contented to drink his fine whiskey as he talked of mundane things. She realized much later that he had not apologized for dragging her from her bed at such an ungodly hour, simply calling a man to take his guest home after about a 45 minute visit. Weird! She wondered what the hell he wanted from her. She was intrigued.

The next morning she went to work. The clients left and she got the tape and set to work transcribing it, but knew she wouldn't finish today. They had come late but she worked on it for the few hours left of her work day, and then she went home, locking up tight before she left.

Luke McNally was off to the courthouse and she to her wine and cigarettes. That night, she showered and put on a silky sensual-feeling nightgown and lay down with her wine and cigarettes, smoking and watching another old movie, this time a love story. She finally fell asleep; it was Friday and she could lie around all day tomorrow if she wanted. She wanted to go to lunch or dinner at the new restaurant downtown and see what it was like. Dinner, she thought. That was always fun and this one had an outdoor patio to enjoy with a view of the ocean. She fell asleep, knowing that she had to clean the apartment tomorrow. It had been far too long now.

Monday morning she was at her desk bright and early to finish the man's transcription, word for word. Thank God he spoke clearly. It was a long tape and it would take at least the rest of the day and she didn't need any of the complications that she sometimes had to put up with. Luke came finally. He walked through the front door and went back to his walnut desk; as usual, he ignored his help first thing in the morning, not even glancing her way as he walked into his office. It always took him time to wake up with reams of coffee first. Many times he'd yell at her to bring him another cup and she would stand up and walk to his office.

"Fuck you McNally. Get your own fucking coffee and don't bother me again if you want me to finish this damned tape." Then she'd huff back to her desk in the other room. The lazy jerk could fire her for all she cared.

She already knew that there were attorneys all over town who would love to get their hands on her, probably because of her rather large boobs but also because of her legal expertise and years of experience, especially now that she had her law degree.

They all had seen her in the courtroom and truly envied McNally. They were certain that was bedding her; not fair, they told him. And he flaunted her, flipping them off as he passed, putting a possessive hand on her back, which she usually slapped away. They would laugh at his humiliation, not really reading him at all; he loved it. They went to court that morning with Jose. Luke insisted that she go and she told him she was going to kick his idiot ass. She did not have time for his stupid dependency on her, but he walked to the outside door and waited. She just ignored them, continuing to type, but he went to her and pulled her out of the chair once again and pushed her to the door.

"Fucking jerk!" She yelled at him, fuming mad. Jose walked with Luke, getting a big, big kick out of the whole scene unfolding before him.

"Good for you, Luke." The halfwit cop killer said. "You know how to treat a woman, Councilor."

She ignored them, surprised the criminal knew what councilor even meant.

The bail hearing took all of 10 minutes, as she knew it would. Jose posted bail and left to whatever the fuck the loser was up to, no good no doubt. He drove them directly to a café while she fumed.

"Hang onto your pataloonies, Danielle. There isn't a damn thing I can do yet. Jose comes first or there will be a major conflict of interest with the Johnsons if I don't move carefully with this one. The father was very likely killed by one of the lynch men for one of the organized crime bosses that Jose is involved with. He couldn't have been as innocent as his family thought or he'd still be alive and well. They're growing stronger by the minute here in South Carolina, and they have their hands in pretty much everything now. The authorities act like they're clueless, but I believe they'll strike a crippling blow against them very soon, and our boy is a very active member." He informed her, as they accepted the menu from the tired old waitress.

"Really? I think that's wonderful news. Maybe they'll kill him." She said, sipping the hot coffee.

"To me, it's quite obvious that Mr. Johnson was killed by someone involved in the organization, and our Jose is way up the rung with them."

"Will you go after them?"

"Of course I will. They killed him and who knows how many others, some perhaps deserving of their deaths because they are also murders and some totally innocent like maybe Leroy Johnson. I'm not sure about that because they obviously targeted him for a reason, probably for the simple fact that he may have pocketed some of their money or kept a few drugs to sell on his own. They just don't go after innocent people like that, but they have to pay for what they did to him and others like him and I'm going to make certain that they do."

"Are you sure McNally? That's going to be damned expensive and we both know how tight you are with all those useless millions laying around for no good purpose."

"Yeah, time to put it to good use for something more than your thieving little fingers." And they ordered.

When she finished the tape, he told her to go home and she did. Nothing to do and it would be nice to just lie around and watch TV, which she did. Then she went to dinner, walking in the dusk of the warm autumn evening, and finally went back home to her wine and cigarettes. She talked to her cousin Leanne, who asked if she could come over tomorrow after work but she told her she would have to wait for weekend and they hung up. Maybe they'd go shopping but neither one of them needed a damned thing, so maybe just lunch or something.

She went back to work and no longer had to struggle to find something to keep herself busy when the office was quiet and there were no clients because McNally was in a trial. All the files had to be re-alphabetized after they had been tossed all over her office floor, so she set to work, glad to have something to do. It would take days she knew. Many of the folders had lost both the tape and the hard copy of the report she had transcribed, laying somewhere in the huge mess of papers and cassette tapes still scattered on the floor, so she had her work cut out for her, thank God. McNally came in and helped her, placing the typed transcription papers in a pile on her desk and then picking up the folders and shuffling through them to try to match the papers with their rightful owner.

"Please Luke, go back to your office. You're taking my work away from me. It's hard enough to find work around here nowadays."

"That's going to end this afternoon. The Barnett's are on their way in. They'll be here in about half an hour, and then another client is coming in right behind them."

"Oh Thank God! You took care of Jose then?"

"Nope. The Cartel just escorted him to Mexico to wait it out."

"The Cartel? Are you sure? Did he tell you that?"

"No, but to me it's very obvious. One minute he was there and kept every appointment without fail, and then he was suddenly nowhere to be seen. They're the big boys who bring the drugs into Chicago and New York City and then they have them distributed to their most trusted longtime employees, people like Jose, who then distributes the drugs to his street people to sell them. He'll have plenty to keep him busy while he's there, that's for sure. He's going to be working overtime just trying to dodge bullets and save his ass from all the gunfire that he's likely going to be facing."

He said, watching her trying to separate the mess all over the floor.

"So who do you think did this?" He asked her, plopping in her office chair and leaning back, his legs on the desk, his arms crossed behind his head. Danielle looked at him. He was so damned good-looking and mean as spit. If she didn't know first-hand what an asshole he was, she would fallen head over heels from the first day. She was going to miss his constant attempts to seduce her she knew. She'd work something out though, maybe work part-time for him. That would surely give him plenty of time to come after her, she thought with a smile, remembering.

"I have my suspicions. Who do you think it was?"

"I think they were after the Johnson transcripts. As I said, I think it was an organized crime boss that put out a hit on him, no doubt about it. His son says he was a good man, and I don't doubt that for a minute, but he must have had his hand in something somewhere or he would be alive right now." He said again, driving his suspicions home once again. "They just don't go after innocent people, except maybe those who unintentionally get in their way."

"But it's right here." She said, picking up the typed transcripts from the floor.

"Where's the tape?"

She looked on the floor at all the cassettes. "I don't have a clue; I've got to listen to them one at a time and then match them up with the transcribed documents.

This time I'm writing the name on every damned one of those cassettes before I match them into the client's folder and file them away."

"Good idea. Probably should have done that from the beginning."

"Yeah, believe me I know."

The door opened and the Barnett family arrived, walking into the reception area and following Luke back to the office. At the door, he turned and said, "I may need you to standby. Probably not, but don't leave. We can order takeout when you're ready."

"Gotcha." She said, gathering all the tapes from the floor and throwing them into her wire basket on the desk. She'd listen to them all throughout the next week and get them back up in the shelf in alphabetical order, another three or four days at least, maybe even longer if there were clients and tapes to transcribe, but she was glad for the work.

The Barnett's finally left; the woman's eyes red and swollen. They were always red Danielle thought as she said good-bye. She had lost a daughter who had been gunned down as she walked to dinner one evening with some friends. The family was adamant that it was her jilted ex-fiancé who had done this. Whether he had an alibi or not, it was him. He had been arrested when his alibi didn't check out but he finally wised up and got an attorney who told him that he should plead not guilty and now they were getting ready for one hell of a trial; the kind that McNally loved, especially because he would likely be on every major news station in the city of Savannah.

It would be terrible to lose someone you loved in such a horribly violent way, Danielle thought. The lovely young lady had definitely been the target as she stood with her friends, and he was the only one who could have done this; however, there was no evidence to point to him, everything was circumstantial and McNally doubted that he would be convicted with what they had on him. His lawyer made it very clear that his client simply panicked when he was questioned by the police, which could certainly be the reason for his bogus alibi. By the time he finally asked for a lawyer he was pretty much screwed, but McNally thought his chances were excellent and he conveyed this to his clients who refused to accept that as fact. It was up to the jury now.

That night, she went to bed early. It was very cold, and she liked to turn on the fireplace and sleep on the couch, but tonight she went into the bedroom, needing the TV to put her to sleep. She turned it to on to the movie channel and was asleep in no time at all. She woke to a very handsome man standing beside her bed, looking down at her. She wondered how long he had been standing there, but he looked completely relaxed and calm as he smiled down at her. Thank God she didn't snore, she thought as she looked into his handsome face. At least she didn't think she did anyway.

"Time to wake up, lovely lady. Someone wants to talk to you. Get dressed." She knew where he was taking her. She dressed quickly, dressing in front of him, not the least bit intimidated by the man's presence. She grabbed her purse as they left the apartment and went to the big Mercedes parked right outside the apartment building. He said nothing and she had no questions. She was wide awake and anxious to meet her distinguished friend once again; he evidently wanted her company for some reason. Probably something to do with McNally. She looked at her watch; again 2:00 a.m. Did that older, but oh-so-attractive gentleman ever sleep, she wondered.

He led her again to the very modern office building and they took the elevator to the penthouse. Who knew? She had no idea Savannah even had penthouses in the city. The kind gentleman waited for them, watching her walk to the couch across from him.

"You go on home to your family now, Alberto, and thank you."

"Thank you, Mr. Anderson. Good night." And then he left, quietly letting himself out.

"You have a lovely office, Mr. Anderson. It's breathtaking."

"Thank you Danielle. It serves its purpose. May I offer you a drink?"

"A glass of wine would be heavenly." She told him again, pulling her cigarettes, hesitating, not sure if he would appreciate the smell of smoke.

She liked looking at the man. He brought her a large crystal ashtray and handed her the wine, and then went back and poured what looked like fine bourbon, McNally's drink of choice of course. He sat down and lit a cigar. He talked to her about her business, both legal and illegal. She said nothing, waiting for the punchline.

"I've been watching you for a very long time now, even before Jose. I've seen you many times in court. I'm certain that you weren't aware of my presence because I always sit in the back of the courtroom. McNally obviously depends on you and since he's the best, that's certainly a good sign." He said, smoking his cigar, completely relaxed.

"I was quite pleased when you decided to go to law school of course. I kept tabs on you and was very pleased that you passed in the top 5% of your class, especially since there were so many people graduating. You are one very smart little lady, as I knew you would be. I'm exceedingly impressed with you. That's why I'm talking to you now. I could use a smart woman like you. I need someone I can trust with my financial endeavors which are many, and I believe you're that person. Are you interested?"

"I'm quite flattered, Mr. Anderson. Of course, I'm very interested. I believe I can handle whatever it is that you need, but it may take some time of course."

"When do you think you might be able to start?"

"Not this Monday, but perhaps the next; certainly by the end of the month if that will work for you. I just have a few more things to clean up and I will very likely have to interview and hire someone to take my place because McNally just doesn't have the time for that."

"I'm told that the Barnett's were there today."

"Yes. They were. There is a tape of the interview that I have to transcribe on Monday."

"Can you get that tape for me?"

"Of course. But I will also be transcribing a hard copy of the interview. That might be better if you're interested. McNally would definitely notice a missing tape." She said, wondering why the hell he was interested in the Barnett transcript.

"Yes, do that and the Johnson transcript also. Put them away until you get your own office where you can file them in a nice safe place. You never know when we'll need it. Okay, well that's it. Let's get you home."

They walked to the elevator and he led her to the garage and handed her off to the limousine parked in the first space beyond the elevator. "Take good care of her, Maurice. Good-night little lady and welcome aboard."

Didn't any of his men ever sleep, she wondered as she got into the spacious car for her ride back home.

When she got home, of course she couldn't sleep. She'd need new clothes, professional clothes to befit her new very important position. She'd go first thing in the morning. Her new very likely illegal life was calling loudly, but she wasn't certain about that. He may only trust her with the legal part of his businesses. She'd just have to wait and see. She was certainly ready for a change in a big, big way. But not with that junk heap she drove. She never bought the new one because she didn't want to hear McNally's shit. He'd be following her, asking her where she got the money, over and over again until he would about drive her insane, but she would definitely do that as soon as possible.

He met her at her beautiful new office one day on her lunch break and introduced her to the women hired to assist her. The young women were dark-haired and very businesslike. And they dressed very professionally, she noticed immediately. Mr. Anderson had said they were quite wild and loved to dance. As she looked at them across the desk; she sincerely doubted that he had the correct information. These women would never kick up their heels, she thought.

She hoped she would be busy. And she was. She had to learn first the legitimate businesses, mostly real estate; she had to brush up on her real estate law. She also would have to immerse herself in the illegal, mostly money laundering and off shore accounts, which he quite openly talked with her about. Damn, talk about trust; this was the ultimate, especially since he really didn't know her. It was fun and she knew she could easily protect her boss' illegal activities with no problem. She had learned a lot in the six years she had been with McNally. She knew she would miss him terribly, but she felt that she was more than ready for this challenge and she looked forward to her new beginnings; but more than anything, she wanted to please her new boss who trusted her for no good reason at all.

She worked six days a week, coming in on Saturday to interview all the applicants. When she got to the office that morning after accepting her new position, she called and placed an ad for a legal transcriptionist in the want ads. She began getting calls a few days later, setting up interviews. There were so many experienced women who wanted the job, some of them quite young and very nice looking which would certainly please McNally.

"What the hell are you doing?" He asked, storming into her office when the last woman had left for the day. "I don't need another transcriptionist, there's not enough work to keep you busy as it is, or at least that's what you keep telling me."

"McNally, I'm going to tell you one more time. Look at me!!! You have just a few more weeks now to make a decision, because I'm walking out that door, so you better get cracking Bud. You need to be here during the interviews or you're going to be in a hell of a mess by the end of the month because there will be no one to transcribe your tapes."

"You never told me that!!"

"And you never listen. I'm warning you, McNally. You better think about it real hard now, you half-wit!"

But he didn't, thinking only that she would change her mind. She was always threatening to leave but she liked stealing his money, so he was pretty confident that she'd be sitting right there, in spite of her silly warnings and threats.

"It's just time now, McNally. I hope we will always be good friends and that you will call on me if you get into a jam. I promise I'll be right there."

"I'll give you a raise."

"No, I have plenty especially now."

"I'll bet." He sneered. "Where will you go?" She just ignored his insult.

"My office is a block from the courthouse."

"Good, at least I can still take you to lunch."

"I would love that, Luke. Just call me or drop by my office, either way is fine with me."

"Okay. That will work great, especially when I need to run something past you with one client or another."

"Yes. But please don't ask me to your bride, McNally."

"Okay."

And she left him, not even glancing back as she shut the door. Finished; time to move on.

The work was exhilarating to her. She was in court often. His people were always getting busted for one thing or another, mostly drugs that were brought to the city for distribution. She had no idea exactly what his role was in any of this, but it was pretty suspicious that she would be instructed go to court to fight for bail for the offender, trying to get it down to as low as possible, and then would post bail as he instructed. Sometimes they disappeared into the crowds of Mexico to wait it out, and sometimes they were never heard from again. She suspected that they had been murdered just like McNally always said, but that was fine with her as long as the body wasn't discovered and identified or the assassins weren't caught and brought to trial, which of course they never were; too professional for something like that to happen. As far as she was concerned, every one of them was a heartless criminal caring only about the almighty dollar, and it didn't seem to bother any of them if other people died at their hands. She reluctantly had to admit that her boss was very likely the head of this very well run criminal enterprise, and even though he was handsome and he was dignity personified, the man would have to be dangerous as hell in order to control something like that.

Men moved in and out of her office, many times taking her or the other women in the office to lunch and trying to get them into their beds; no one in the office was interested, but they still came, apparently happy to just look at the beauties. These men were dangerous, very likely lynch men for her boss and they were no one to mess with they all agreed.

Mr. Jan Anderson would come in frequently just to take her to lunch and talk business. She was always ready when he shot questions at her and she knew he was damned impressed, which was her goal. With time, she would join his family for brunch or dinner parties. He appeared to be proud of her. She was pretty certain that a man his age would never be able to sustain an erection unless he was on some kind of medication, but a man's tongue always worked she knew, no matter what the age. She had never done anything like that, but if he wanted to do that to her, she wasn't going to discourage it. She had been a virgin far too long now and she certainly wasn't saving herself for any particular reason. She simply hadn't had the opportunity outside of McNally and his idiot clients, which she would never consent to under any circumstances. She wanted a real man, not a half-wit.

"Do you have lovers or anyone who interests you, Danielle?" He asked her at lunch one day. It had been a long day and she just wanted to drink, which he was always willing to accommodate.

"No one in particular. Of course there are always temptations. The Italians are quiet aggressive, so yes there are temptations.

"Have you bedded anyone yet?"

"Hell no! I don't want to be shot. If nothing else, there's a girlfriend or a wife lurking, watching for the right time to extract revenge with a gun."

He laughed. "Be careful beautiful lady, I have my eyes on you, and my fat little Celeste is quite jealous, I have to warn you. But I'd protect you so that she'd never even guess."

"Well you just let me know, boss. I'll even bring the Viagra."

"Oh my goodness. I've think I've just been insulted."

"No!" She laughed, getting up and sitting in his lap. "I'm just going by what I've heard."

"I'm going to surprise, you my beautiful lawyer, and he did. He started slowly, coming into the office late and waiting for the girls to leave. He took her to the couch and stripped her clothes until she stood naked and then he would lay her down and admire her before pouring them a drink as he sat across from her in his recliner. She didn't mind being naked one bit. The office was warm and the door was locked, and then he'd join her, making her scream with his tongue just as she had hoped he would. The man knew exactly what to do and she loved it, anxiously waiting for the next encounter. When he finished with her, he would kiss her sweetly and then escort her to her car. He did need Viagra she thought, but she sure didn't want to insult him again. This was just fine she'd think as she got dressed. She was hungry and her favorite hotel dining room was calling out to her. She'd eat and then go out to the beach and walk barefooted in the sand looking at the moon. She knew she was being watched and she loved it. He was protecting her, she knew.

With time, he'd take off his clothes as soon as she was satisfied. He was quiet well-endowed and he knew exactly how to use that lovely, lovely penis, pounding into her like any young buck. He didn't ask if she was a virgin when he saw the small amount of blood and she didn't volunteer any information in that department. Then he'd get dressed and kiss her once again before calling it a night.

She loved his family. He was Scandinavian, but he had married a very short, very fat Italian woman. He had 2 young daughters who loved their horses, but neither were particularly attractive, looking very much like a younger version of their mother, but you just never knew, she'd think, watching them when she was invited to join the family. A little plastic surgery and they would quite possibly end up being far prettier than they were right now, if they would even care about such things that is. His three sons would many times join them with their sultry wives who they kept pregnant, just not barefooted. They had a million expensive shoes in their closets, the men would say at dinner. With time, he took her to the south of France and then Italy and Spain. She loved the man so much and she told him often, so happy. He would of course ignore her, and just give her a weak smile, which was absolutely fine with her.

McNally came around often, taking her to lunch. Many times she'd meet him at the courthouse and they'd wander down the street to one of the endless outdoor cafés or hotels on the beach.

"Why in God's name didn't you tell me you were an attorney? I need you, you rotten bitch. I can't believe you did this to me. You know that I would have paid you a huge salary. You could have bought yourself a penthouse just like your boss'." He had been there many times when he defended one of his men.

"I know you're fucking him." He told her at dinner one night. "Can the old man even get it up? And why him and not me? I was always good to you, letting you steal my money and make a damn fool of me."

"I made a damn fool of you? How exactly did I make a fool out of fucking fool? Is that even possible?"

"Just tell me why?"

"He curls my toes and he knows how to approach a woman. Not like a bull in a china closet, McNally. You have no idea how this man can turn me on, and the man is huge. He makes your dick look like a little boys."

"Oh thanks." He said, taking a huge drink of his whiskey."

She got up and sat in his lap and kissed him. "Sorry baby. I promise you that you are first in my heart, I mean it McNally. I adore you, little dick and all."

"Great." He said. And then they left, he to his office and she to hers. She was being followed still, she knew, and every word she said was very likely being written down, but of course she didn't mind. She knew Jan trusted her because she had certainly never given him any reason to doubt her loyalty, and she appreciated that he had her watched every minute of the day. She still had her privacy, but she always felt safe and even loved as she moved about the city.

One autumn day, Jan called her to his penthouse. He poured the drinks and sat in the big recliner, and she in her usual place on the couch.

"How's McNally? I am very much aware that you see him quite often."

"Yes. I love my old boss, Jan. Please don't even give it a thought. You're my only true love."

They hadn't made love in a long time, but of course she didn't mind. When he was ready, he'd come to her. They talked of the upcoming horse race that his young daughters were involved in. She wasn't invited but she wasn't particularly interested in that kind of thing anyway.

"Where's McNally?" she asked Jan a month later.

"I have no answer to that question, Danielle. I couldn't possibly know what the man does when he's not in court or where he's gone off to."

She was concerned. He didn't answer his phone or show up to any of his court hearings. She had gone to his office, but he was never there, the office was deserted looking and it felt sad to her without McNally's presence, sitting at his desk and smoking his cigars. His spiffy new Mercedes sat in the parking lot right outside the door where he always parked. The engine was cold and she knew it hadn't been moved since the day he disappeared into thin air. She had called hospitals and jails, but he was nowhere. She went to the police department and made a missing person's report.

She had to find him. She couldn't live without him. Maybe he finally went to the countries he always wanted see, but she doubted that; there was no way that man would walk out on his clients that where scheduled for trial. She knew that McNally would never even consider such a thing; his reputation was far too important to him to ever do anything that might jeopardize his pristine reputation as a criminal lawyer. She'd wait and if he didn't come back soon, she was going to start looking for him on her own, and she would not stop until she found him and brought him back home. She should have never left that fool; she knew that this was her fault and that Jan was to blame for this. She checked McNally's account often; she knew the bank accounts by heart and had for years. Nothing. What the fuck! The lousy bastard had better call her! She couldn't concentrate at work and she took many days off, not wanting to miss his call, although she always had her cell phone with her and he could easily reach her, but he might need her. She couldn't sleep.

When Jan took her to lunch a month later, she asked him again.

"I know you know where Luke is Jan. Just tell me."

"I can't help you with that one." He said casually.

"You're a fucking liar Jan. Do you really think I'll let you get by with this?"

"You love him." He stated, looking at her across the small table.

"You're goddamned right I love him, you lousy son-of-a-bitch. I'm not going to let you get by with this."

"Oh really? And what is it you'll do, if you don't mind my asking?"

"For beginners, I'm going to let your wife and daughters know all about us."

"Be very careful little lady. You have no idea who you're talking to."

"Oh but I do. Do you really think I'm afraid of you, Jan? You are nothing to me. I'll slit your throat before you even know what hit you. I'm Mexican; I know how to use a knife, a switch blade, a piece of broken glass, whatever's handy. Keep that in mind while you're begging your fat dumpy wife not to leave you and take all your money."

"Go home little girl. I don't want to have to hurt you. You're my favorite little whore, but I will not hesitate to deal with you harshly if you carry out your threats against my family."

And she got up and walked away, leaving him sitting there in the restaurant by himself. She no longer felt the endless eyes watching her. She went back to the office and fired her assistants and then closed the doors, taking all the important client files, including Barnett and Johnson and anything else she could get her hands on that proved he was a crook.

In spite of the very clear threat Jan had made, she went straight to Celeste and told her everything while the poor sweet woman cried, but she didn't feel bad at all, just wanting revenge for what he had done to McNally.

"No, Celeste." She said, putting her arms around the short and very plump woman. "No amount of money is worth this. Get a divorce and just have fun with your lovely daughters." She said, hoping that would be exactly what she'd do. But of course she didn't. She had known that he had other women for years now. He always brought them to the house and she would know. All so lovely, not old and fat like her, and she would sigh and try to ignore what was right in front of her. He was a good husband and he was a wonderful father to their children. He took care of his family and that was all she needed for her and her children.

She went to the Johnson house and talked to the family. They hadn't known that McNally was missing. The young son, Marvin, vowed to help her.

"Please call me."

"I will. Please be available if I need you. I've got to find him, and maybe with both of us working on it together, we'll be able to find a clue that will lead me to him."

"I will. I'm right here." But he wasn't. He was killed in a car accident a short time later. Sure he was, she thought, so fucking angry she couldn't even eat.

She talked to the Feds, flying personally to the FBI headquarters in Washington DC. She had document after document of the money laundering and the off shore accounts, which she turned over to a very handsome

Italian agent. He took her to lunch and they strategized. Then they went back to the office. He asked her for every possible thing she could think of. What did McNally look like, and she handed him a picture that one of her friends had snapped of him in the courthouse hall as he walked out of the courtroom and she had videos of him standing in front of a microphone talking to the news about one of his clients that he was defending. She knew approximately how long he had been missing, on and on, trying desperately to remember anything that might help to find him. She knew everything there was to know about the man, but it didn't seem to make one bit of difference. The agent promised that he would find him if he was still alive and if he wasn't, they would bring his body to her, and they parted ways. But she didn't go home. No fucking way was she going to walk straight to certain death. She had to find McNally, and maybe with the help of the FBI, she would be able to do just that.

She found an apartment as close to Quantico as she could possible get where she felt quite safe as she searched the internet for some sort of clue until her fingers were sore, many times falling asleep at the small desk, but she had no idea what she was looking for or where to begin. What was she going to do? She had never been a religious woman, but she was now. She went to the cathedral every morning and lit candles, talking directly to God, knowing that the Virgin Mary wasn't strong enough for something like this. She had never really believed that the woman had the power she was believed to have anyway. God was the man to talk to now. And she waited and waited. What God? Please tell me what to do, she would beg.

Morgan informed her the next morning that charges had been brought up against Jan and that he had been arrested. She wondered who the bastard's lawyer was, certainly not her, of course. She would have gotten him off in a New York's second. Too bad so sad. She hoped that he rotted in hell and that Celeste spent every dollar of his hard-earned money.

She decided to move to the comfortable hotel near the FBI offices, not far from her old apartment. She felt better in the crowds and the safety of the busy hotel suite. She traveled under a fake passport and ID and had moved her money from savings immediately. She certainly did learn a lot from Jan and his money laundering that was for sure, but of course hers was a sad drop in the bucket compared to his billions, but still it was hers and she fully intended to keep it for a rainy day.

After dinner, she wanted to go outside and walk even though it was freezing cold. She was so full she could barely move her fat body. It was only 6:00 but it was winter dark and cold as hell as the wind blew off the Potomac. When she exited the lobby of the hotel to the sidewalk, it was freezing and the wind had picked up sharply, the storm very likely blowing in from the Atlantic or some such place, but she didn't mind. She never felt it;

her sad and lonely thoughts were only on her McNally. Was he cold, she wondered? God please protect him. But she knew he was dead. He had been gone too long; people like Jan didn't leave witnesses, but a witness to what? She couldn't think what it might be. He didn't strike her as a jealous man, and she had assured him that their relationship was nothing, but that had to be the reason; what else could it be? He did this; she knew beyond any shadow of a doubt that Jan was responsible for this. All that was left for her now was to find his body, she thought, so damned sad, remembering what a bastard he had been; so full of confidence, so full of life. She had always loved him, even though it was simple good old fashioned lust on his part of course, but she'd take that any day to this. She wished with all her heart that she had allowed him to do the things he would tell her he planned for her. It had disgusted her virgin heart then, but now....she would give anything to have him talking his disgusting talk now.

She decided that as soon as she got back to Savannah, she'd go to Jan and offer to disappear, to not testify against him if it came to that, if he would just tell her where the body was; she very likely was going to be the only witness to take the stand against her former employee and lover, and he might agree to tell her. He may very well just murder her and bury her body in a shallow grave, but she had to try. She often wondered why it was so important to her to bury McNally, but for some unknown reason, it meant everything to her.

There were few people on the sidewalks that usually had quite a lot of pedestrians walking past the hotel from the large parking structure at the end of the block. No one wanted to be out in this cold. Christmas decorations lined the boulevard and the store windows had mechanical Christmas Santa Clauses and elves busily making toys and packing Santa's sled for Christmas Eve. DC went all out for Christmas, at least in this section of town. She wondered if the streets of Savannah were decorated for the holiday. She had never noticed. Life had been too busy to celebrate Christmas or Thanksgiving or even her birthday. She hadn't had a Christmas tree or a Christmas present since her grandmother had died she realized.

She wore a thick sweater and blue jeans, something she had never done before, too busy trying to impress to ever dress in such attire. She had never even owned a pair of the heavy denim pants; too hot for the rather warm days of winter in Savannah. She'd have to buy a coat tomorrow if she planned to stay any longer with the FBI. Morgan had told her that this was only the beginning and there was much left to do. She had assured him today that of course she would be here for the long run. She turned left from the lobby doors and walked slowly down the dark boulevard, but the Christmas lights on the poles lit up the sidewalk beautifully, twinkling brightly through the snow as it fell. Her arms were folded against her chest as she walked, barely aware of the sharp cold wind as it swirled the snow softly around her.

She walked down the street slowly; the blizzard that had been predicted was definitely here now. It was freezing without a coat, but she wore her very warm sweater which helped a little. She'd go tomorrow and buy more sweaters and a coat, she promised herself once again as she walked, but just to the corner. The streets were pretty much empty of anyone, but she felt safe. But she wasn't safe.

She walked to corner and turned back. She was suddenly, unexpectedly and very violently dragged into a dark doorway. A big man punched her in the face immediately and then began to choke her, his big meaty hands chocking the life from her; she weaved in and out of consciousness as she fought. She knew this wasn't a robbery attempt. The man intended to kill her quickly, leaving her body there in that dark, cold doorway when he was finished with her and then he would simply walk away into the storm. Jan! His name was screaming in her head as she fought to stay on her feet. She instinctively lifted her knee as hard as she could into his groin. She had made contact, thank God, thank God. She kicked him in the face with her heavy hiking boots when he fell to his knees and ran as fast as her long slender legs would carry her back to the safety of her room.

Her right eye was black and had closed completely shut within minutes. She hadn't put ice on it because she didn't know that you were supposed to do that. All she wanted was wine and her precious cigarettes. She called room service and ordered 4 bottles of champagne. A very handsome young man brought the silver bucket filled with the bottles and sat them onto the table in front of the couch where she sat.

"Are you okay Danielle?" He asked, the concern evident in his voice.

"Yes, I'm fine, Ron, nothing a little liquor won't make better." Mugged right outside the hotel, she said to her young friend as he handed her the tall champagne flute. He had been there since the beginning to serve her in the evenings and they had become fast friends. He was also enrolled in law school.

"We have a small clinic right here in the hotel. Why don't I call the doctor? He'll come directly to your room tonight." He said.

"No, Ron. I'm fine. I've got an appointment tomorrow morning. I'll see him after that."

He left and she drank until the wee hours. She'd talk to Morgan and then she'd go shopping for winter clothing she decided as she finally changed into her pajamas and climbed into bed.

"Wow." Morgan said as she sat down. "What the hell happened to you?"

"Too much champagne and too many doors."

"I'd sue, Madame Attorney." He joked.

"Yeah, I plan to." She shot back.

"Who was it?"

"I don't have a clue, only guesses."

"Our friend Mr. Anderson isn't going to stop, you know."

"How in the hell did he find me? He can't possibly know my alias."

"Of course he can. The man keeps track of everything that concerns him or his businesses; that's how he's survived this long. There's no going back once a person is on his list. I'd be willing to bet he knew your alias as soon as you bought it; the man has eyes everywhere and you can bet that the man who gave you that alias was someone Mr. Anderson knew, maybe even his employee."

"I know you're right. I knew his history when he hired me as his personal attorney. I knew everything when I walked into my beautiful new office. I knew all the ins and outs of his money laundering within a week. Did you get the money from the offshore accounts?"

"Yes ma'am that is why you may not live to grow very much older." He informed her, his legs on his desk, his arms behind his head, reminding her sadly of McNally so long ago.

"Yep. I knew that when I decided to go to the FBI. I'm going back now Morgan. Time to start looking closer to home."

"No. You can't."

"Yes sir I can. The only way you'll ever be able to stop me is to toss my ass in jail or get me pregnant. That might work."

"It's tempting, my lovely dark haired vixen, but Mom wouldn't like it."

"I'm leaving in the morning. What I need from you this minute is a new ID. Obviously my old one is comprised."

He picked up the phone and gave the order. "Yes, I'll tell her. She's sitting right here. Okay, thanks. Just give me a call when it's ready. Yes, she'll be right down. Do something about her black eye and the swelling if you can." And he hung up.

"Okay, the photographer is waiting."

"See ya."

As soon as she walked out the door, Morgan began making arrangements for Witness Protection for his witness. Without her testimony, nothing would ever be done to stop this monster.

He took many pictures as she sat in a chair under a rather bright light.

"I need for you to make me a blond with short curly hair and blue eyes."

"Sure. No problem. Just don't get on a flight until you've disguised yourself." He told her.

"I'm going to get the things I need for the new me as soon as I leave here. Thank you for your expertise. When can I pick it up?"

"This afternoon. This is a stat photo. And I suggest to you that you get some dark sun glasses too. The winter sun and even bright lights can be brutal to someone in your condition." The photographer told her. It was true; her eye was pulsating and watering painfully from the photographers very bright lights.

She left and went immediately to the department store, but of course they had no wigs or anyway for her to change her eye color. She bought large round and very dark sunglasses and went back to the hotel; she ate a wonderful breakfast and then went to her hotel suite and lay down again. She was drained. When she woke, she went to the desk and pulled the yellow pages. She'd start with the optometrist and then the wig shop. She called a cab and went directly to the optometrist. He examined her and then she bought medium blue contacts, but he warned her not to try to put them in until her eye had a chance to heal a little more, maybe a day or two, he said. From there she bought a curly, short blond wig that would fit perfectly as soon as she had her thick long hair cut short, but she didn't hesitate for one second even though she had never in her life had anything but her waist long hair. Evidently Mexican's didn't cut their hair. It had never occurred to her to do such a thing actually.

They gave her clips to hold it to her head, showing her how to secure it. From there she went straight to the beauty shop in the hotel and had her beautiful, never cut hair taken off almost to the scalp. It shocked her that she had soft curls, like a cap covering her head. Who knew? She decided this was the way she would always wear her hair. She thought she looked cute as could be. Then she went back to the FBI headquarters and picked up her ID, wearing her wig, but not her contacts. Her eye was no longer as swollen as it had been, but it was extremely tender and the eye itself was quite red.

"I've gotten you into Witness Protection. We need to keep you alive for the hearing."

"Yes, that would be very nice. Thanks again, Morgan. I honestly hope to see you again."

"I wouldn't miss it, Danielle. It shouldn't be much longer now."

As soon as she landed in Savannah, she rented a car and drove to the bank and closed out her accounts, and then went to a new bank and got an account under her new name. She then drove to her old office, McNally's office. It was so dusty and she needed to get busy. There was a lot to do before she moved in. She knew there was a broom and some furniture polish but that was it, so she locked up, thankful that she hadn't even thought to give McNally her key, and he never did ask for it either. The first thing she did was have the utilities turned back on in the office, and then she drove downtown. It was time to buy clothes befitting a just out of school young attorney. She had found a small bottle that contained eye drops in Luke's desk and applied it her damaged eye. The redness and soreness disappeared by the next afternoon, even though the skin around her eye was now a dark green with some purple bruising; she knew that it would take time, but she had the glasses. She would wait to put in the blue contacts until she no longer needed the sunglasses. She drove to the department store, where she bought some very nice sandals in black and brown and even white to match the pedal pushers and the bright short-sleeved summer blouses. From there she went to the sheets and found two flat sheets; fitted sheets would be useless on a couch. She found the pillows and pillow cases and also purchased a very soft blanket. She stopped at the makeup counter and let the girl do her makeup, buying all the products. She was amazed at the difference now, the bruise hidden under the thick green makeup that the girl had used around the bruised skin; it was outrageously expensive for such a small jar, but she certainly didn't care. From there it was to the jewelry counter where she bought a lovely platinum watch, the face surrounded by small diamonds, and then a very small and delicate chain that had small diamonds scattered all the way around the chain. She was finished now. She paid with the credit card that had her new name on it and left. Next was the gun shop. She found a very nice Glock that wasn't too heavy. The clerk helped her to fill out the security papers for the security check and told her it shouldn't be more than a couple of weeks, a month at the most. Then he signed her up for shooting lessons and the indoor shooting range in the next building. From there she went to the newspaper and placed an ad for her new business to run for a full month. If it generated business, she would run it for as long as she needed it. Then she went home to wait. She called yellow pages to have her business added there too. Friday was the cutoff date, so she had called just in time the man told her as he took her information.

"When will the new books be delivered?"

"In a couple of months." Perfect.

She pulled her cleaning products from the bag and got to work so happy to have something to do. She worked all day and into the next afternoon until the rooms shone and glistened. Then she called a paint contractor who met her at the office that afternoon. They went over all the colors on the chart and she chose her favorite color for the main room to run in a lighter color of the same shade in the big office. She got in her car and went to Sears and purchased a big very expensive rug from India with muted colors of blue and cream. It would be absolutely beautiful in the front office and she thought she was ready to see clients now.

As she waited, she cleared the files from the wall behind the desk and packed them into boxes, and then she drove to storage, making sure that nothing had been compromised during her absence. It hadn't. She locked up and drove to lunch and wine. She wasn't hungry, but she needed to eat. She went back to the office where two men were busy with paint brushes. The key to the office sat on the desk and she put it back on the key ring, reminding herself to have more made. When they finished, she paid the owner of the business and walked the rooms slowly. She adored it. She knew Luke would hate it with a passion. Luke hated anything that wasn't his idea, actually. Tough shit you bastard she thought. It was compensation for all the shit he had put her through. She wanted to cry. She would give anything to be insulted by that asshole now, remembering his total disregard for her as the over-sexed pig tried to slip his disgusting penis into her mouth and as he happily tried his best to assault the young virgin. She would give anything to have him back, even as disgusting as he had been, a caveman and a damned fool; but she would happily embrace all of that now. She didn't sleep well that night, but she had plenty of wine and cigarettes to keep her company.

The next day, she went to the local appliance store and ordered the biggest TV she could find, and made an appointment for a service crew to come out and brace it to the wall in the back office so that she could watch it from the couch when she couldn't sleep. She was ready now, well not quite but almost. With time, Danielle realized that she was not going to be ready to see anyone for a very long time, but she didn't know that at the moment, always thinking she was almost ready but not quite.

She went to breakfast at an outside café and called AT&T to have the telephone turned on since it had of course been turned off for lack of payment for a year now. Where on earth had the time flown off to, she wondered. She'd have to go back to the yellow pages and newspaper and get those changed to the new number today without fail, not even certain why the hell she hadn't thought of that right away. She just didn't think about the fact that the old service had been turned off long ago, along with the electricity.

Now she was pretty certain that she was truly ready. When it was time to go to court, she would buy dresses and heels then, but for now, she had no idea if she would even have a client, let alone go to court.

As she waited for her food at an outdoor café across the street from Mr. Jan Anderson's penthouse, she watched the street and the drivers. Jan never came here, but she was ready if he did. From a car, she knew that he would never recognize her, only that she was a blond, blue-eyed woman, especially since the man had no idea his little attorney had come back to Savannah. She ate slowly and then ordered coffee as she planned how to move forward. Business was as dead as the office she waited in. Everything that needed to be done in the office had been done so she now had all the time in the world to watch Jan's penthouse and even follow the men who came out. She would have to change cars every few days, but she knew they would deliver it to her if she was in a hurry.

She got up and went to a big Barns and Noble on the avenue. She spent the afternoon choosing hard bound leather volumes and atlases. She gave her address to have them all delivered by tomorrow afternoon. She didn't want to wait. The penthouse called her name.

She went back to the department store and bought lovely crystal décor of every color for the file cabinet shelves, now painted a lovely soft color. She would place the leather bound books on one shelf and then the crystals here and there on every shelf along with pots of green ivy. It would be beautiful. They were extremely expensive, almost as much as the books, but who cared. She had Luke's money now too. Nothing was ever a problem or too expensive for her now.

She had no intentions of taking on too much just yet. Her search for Luke was far more important than having clients. She would only accept cases that would be held in civil court. She was pretty certain that Jan would know her the minute he heard her voice. She also knew that he spent an inordinate amount of time in the criminal court to watch and learn, so she'd have to be careful, especially since civil court was in the same building as criminal court. But her biggest duty was to find Luke's body. His money couldn't help him now, she thought so sad she didn't want to lift her head. She went home and drank and waited. Soon now, she thought.

On the way home she passed Home Depot. She realized she didn't have a ladder and went in. She bought a little giant because it would fit in her car easily and she could pull it to a lot of different lengths if she needed to. And then she saw all the lovely hanging baskets and bought enough to run along the little porch just outside the office. When she got home, she hung the beautiful flowering baskets with large hooks that she tried to screw into the eaves along the narrow but long porch. But it was really quite difficult to get the hooks started because she didn't have a drill to start the holes, so she ran back to Home Depot. She stayed busy all afternoon, climbing up and down the ladder as she drilled, and then she would get down for a flower basket and climb back up. She wanted her place of business, her new home now, to be as lovely as possible, whether clients came or not. When she had finished, she walked the asphalt parking lot that began as soon as a person stepped off the porch. This wouldn't do she thought. She called a small construction company and they came to look at the parking lot that afternoon. After they left she looked for the keys to the Mercedes but couldn't find them. He probably had them on him when he was taken, so she called a tow truck and had it moved to a far corner of the lot.

They came the next day to start the excavation of the black asphalt, cutting it away from the area she wanted to turn into a small front yard. Then they bricked off the space between the soil and the asphalt and ran a sidewalk up to the little porch, which was also laid with soft tumbled stone and made to run the full length of her lovely narrow porch, so lovely against the bright color of the flowers that hung above. The yard looked pretty bleak at the moment, but that wouldn't last long she knew.

She called a landscaping company to have sprinklers placed on each side of the now softly muted color of the path of the sidewalk and along the porch. The lawn man wouldn't be there until morning, so she ran back to Home Depot and got a gallon of white paint, brushes, rollers and paint tins to hold her paint. Her ass was on fire from the ladder, so she went inside and turned on TV, pouring wine and smoking a cigarette. She watched Law and Order and then Rizzoli and Isles. She loved these old reruns. She drank, smoked and watched. She had no Advil, and her face was pounding and her head began to hurt. She got up and went to the drugstore and then to an early dinner. The Advil started working almost immediately and she felt almost normal in no time at all. She left the restaurant and walked, remembering Washington DC. She moved slowly and carefully, watching the men's faces as she walked. The men watched her, turning around as she passed some walking backyards as they watched her ass. She ignored them and kept going, lost in thought as she stopped to look in the store front windows. She walked to the drug store, buying more Advil, champagne, cigarettes and something snacky to tide her over. Then she went back home to her TV.

In the morning, she went into the small bathroom and warmed a wash cloth. The damn place had no shower, only a sink and she knew that this would never do. She had developed an obsessive compulsive disorder that had started in her childhood as she watched her pretty mama who also very likely had the same disorder. She absolutely would not live without a way to scrub away the daily dirt and germs. She called the construction company back and showed them the small space. She wanted a large bathroom with a large shower. She also needed a kitchen. He drew what he thought she wanted and she was quite pleased. He gave her a price and left. He told her that he had a small crew available that could start in the morning. She rose early and dressed. She had a Keurig but no pods. She drove to the supermarket and bought the pods and powdered cream and sugar in case a client wanted her coffee doctored up; if she ever had any that is, and then she went to a furniture store and bought a long table that was meant for a hallway; it was made of mirrored glass and would hold the Keurig and pods and coffee cups perfectly and a large bouget of flowers that she would have delivered by a florist maybe once a week or so, depending on how long they lasted. She rearranged all her coffee essentials and then she waited.

The landscaping company was there when she drove up. She told the two tanned, very gorgeous young hunks what she wanted and waited for the construction crew who drove up as she spoke to the hunks and they began to install a sprinkler system and then the landscapers brought the small truck and dumped beautiful dark soil into the space that was to be her yard. They would spread the soil and lay the sod tomorrow after the sprinklers were installed they told her. Once they got busy, she left for Home Depot.

She chose a nice refrigerator with an ice maker and a separate door for fruit and snacks, found a matching electric range and washer and dryer to be delivered in to the construction crew that would work on the kitchen. Then she bought more flowers, accepting the offer for a Home Depot card. She went back to the office, staying in the front office and rearranging her shelves to be perfect, moving books and trinkets and potted ivy to a more pleasing position in the shelves. The landscapers were finished and they started the sprinklers, turning them on low and then turned them off. Don't turn them off for a while once the sod is in place and then you need to leave it on low day and night for a few days, and then they left. She went back in to check on the project. The wall wasn't coming down of course; her new bathroom and kitchen would simply be attached to the outside wall and a hallway built, with lots of windows of course. She forgot tile for the kitchen and bathroom and the glass tile for the shower wall, but that could wait. She was hungry and she was tired.

She went to the hotel dining room and sat out on the patio in the warm afternoon sun. It was late September already and the beautiful weeks of autumn were just around the corner. They had predicted hurricanes this season, and she supposed that was possible since the season lasted until the end of November, but she lived a few miles from the beach, so no worries and it certainly had been quiet up until now. Anyway, all she had to do was huddle until the storm passed. She rented a hotel room upstairs because there was no way she was going to sleep in all that dust, remembering her asthma as a child. The doctor had told her mother to stop cleaning everything so spotlessly and let the tiny girl play outside daily. She did, as she watched her little girl from the window, sometimes playing with her cousins as her auntie visited her mommy. That was happy times for the little girl, she remembered. She wondered where they all were now. Her mother had died of breast cancer in her mid-thirties, and she never saw the aunt or cousins again. Evidently her aunt didn't care for her grandmother, Abigail Maria Herrera, who was the only person to come forward and take the child. Only her uncle stayed in touch with his mother, and she wondered how her younger cousin was doing. She hadn't seen her for a very long time now. She loved her grandmother with all her heart. She was spry and happy and loved to shop. She died when Danielle was in 11th grade, and she continued to live in the house until it went into foreclosure and was sold out from under her. She knew that the real estate lady was going to call social services because she was under age but she took her grandmother's car and slept on quiet residential streets until she could find a job which was how she ended up working for Nasty McNally. She got her own apartment with time even though she had been so young, but she worked and paid the rent easily from the money she started stealing from her boss. A girl had to live for heaven's sake. She would have starved to death on what he paid her, even less than minimum wage, she remembered, smiling, wanting to cry again. Such a damned tightwad! But she had been so young, he had gotten away with it for quite a while and then she'd had enough of his nonsense. He ended up paying very, very well though, she thought with a grin. She thought about her Luke day and night. She'd give anything to have him assaulting her once again. What a lousy no good jerk he had been. He had absolutely no respect for women in general; he told her that women were good for one thing and one thing only so many times. She had to find him. She didn't want to live without him. She wanted him to be alive more than she had ever wanted anything in her life, but that seemed like an impossibility after all this time with absolutely no word from him.

She went back to Home Depot on her way to the office. She was truly fed up with the place, but she knew where everything was now. She found tile and the floors she wanted and paid for them with her credit card. A crew would come next week and put everything down for her. She forgot to order shower doors and shower hardware, so she headed back into the store, turning around in the parking lot. She also needed a sink and faucet for the kitchen. Her damned ass still hurt like hell and she needed to get home to her Advil.

It was almost done. She paid the construction owner and they left. She turned off the sprinkler system; her sod was soaking wet and she was afraid she'd drown her grass before it ever had a chance to take root. It was time to clean again she thought as she walked back into her new home. As she scrubbed and dusted, pulling the new vacuum cleaner from the closet, her phone rang. She answered it with her new name.

"This is Penelope Scott." She said, sounding extremely professional as she grabbed her pad and a pen from the drawer. There was a woman on the line, a very unhappy woman to boot, she was her kind of woman, she thought as she listened and wrote. She gave her name and got right down to business. Her husband was cheating and she wanted a PI to follow him so that she could divorce his cheating ass once she had the proof.

"I can certainly help you with that. You give me the name of his girlfriend and a good picture of your husband and I will follow him." The woman on the phone was pissed, a very nasty lady as far as she could tell. She said she would bring her a picture of her husband and told her she wanted to get the son-of-a-bitch. Penelope asked her for times and dates of the various places he would go, and she shot off the addresses from memory. She knew them all, but she was a mother and she had a job and this was all she could do right now.

Penelope gave her an hourly wage and she they hung up. Her first job, she thought. This was going to work out just fine and dandy. They set a time for the next afternoon and she hung up. She just had a few more things to complete and then she hopped into the shower, washing the wig and putting it on the Styrofoam head to dry for the next day. Before the woman was due to arrive, she applied her makeup with the little machine that shot ivory makeup over her face. All she had to do was add a little blush, mascara to her long thick eyelashes and put on some lipstick. She placed the wig on her head, and she was ready.

Maria Romana was stunning with beautiful hazel cat eyes and tiny features under thick black waves. She had a picture of a tall very sexy Italian son-of-a-bitch with a sexy grin and she had addresses to every bar, girlfriend, and motel he would take them to, then she left, telling her that she had many girlfriends, and just as many fucking Italian husbands who were cheating.

"I sure as hell hope you're ready for this, little lady. You will definitely have your work cut out for you." She said, heading for the door.

"You bet I am. We can file charges as soon as the pictures are developed, then we'll set a court date. You'll get everything your little heart desires and more."

"Yep. Count on it. Just don't let him pull you into his trap too. He'd go after you so fast it would make your blond curls spin." And then she walked out the door.

Penelope turned on her computer. She was extremely rusty on the divorce laws so she needed to get reacquainted now before the fun started. She wrote down settlements and monies awarded next to the woman's name and then started a file. She was ready. Maria was instructed to call her the second her husband left with the address of his current lover.

Then she headed for the camera shop and listened to the advice of the man who waited on her. She bought a Raspberry PI special and all the accessories. She would need a zoom lens. She went home and waited for the call, flipping on the sprinklers as she walked through because the grass had definitely dried out now. She would begin renting different cars now so that she wouldn't be noticed as she followed her target, but this one would do just fine for now.

She went to lunch across the street from her used to be lover's penthouse and took along a big atlas as she watched the entrance. She watched as the gangsters entered the big doors to the fancy lobby. Every one of them was familiar, but they never came back out. They must be exiting through the back entrance to the garage. She was tired now and she wanted wine, so she went home to her sparkling house. She turned off the sprinklers and decided she wanted small flowering trees in the front yard, one on each side of the sidewalk. She'd find a nursery in the morning. She thought that she was very likely going to be busy this evening since it was the weekend, and she was.

She drove to the "whore's" address and parked beneath her 2nd story apartment front door, then changed her mind and parked directly across the parking lot from his SUV. They came out after about half an hour. No wonder Maria was jealous as hell. She was gorgeous but she sure as hell didn't hold a candle to this fake busted, fake lipped escort. She ought to introduce her to Jan she thought. She sure wouldn't be living in this dump for long.

She snapped pictures in the dark, covering the flash as best she could and then followed them to the disco, taking more pictures as they danced and she drank wine. From there she followed them to a small hotel on the strip. There was no way to see anything through the heavily draped window, but she got plenty of before and after pictures as they held hands and walked to SUV. He threw her against the driver's door and kissed her passionately clutching her huge fake breasts in his very big, very hairy hands. His sex drive must be insatiable to be acting like that, even after obviously having sex at least twice that day. Perfect she thought. She waited for them to leave and then drove to the photo shop and dropped the film in the night box with her card. She'd get them tomorrow. She didn't call Maria; she'd deliver the photos as soon as they were ready. The next morning, she filled out the paperwork to start divorce proceedings and then made sure she had a tape in the recorder and plenty of paper for the typewriter and expensive copy machine. God bless Luke. He was cheap but he certainly did buy the best. Uh, well.... thanks to her of course, while he bitched and strutted in front of her like a fucking rooster harassing the stupid little hen. She laughed. He was something; he always had been. She had adored him within the first month of her employment, mostly because he was the brightest goof she had ever known. She decided that it was time to buy a computer. She had had one when she worked for Jan but it never occurred to her to purchase one for herself until now.

She left and went to breakfast, ordering a bloody Mary with her omelet and coffee in the little outside café directly across the street from the penthouse. She watched but saw no one. Then she saw Jan pull up and hand the key to his Mercedes to the waiting valet and disappear into the lobby. She sipped and read and waited for the crew. When they came in two by two, she went to the underground garage, her camera ready. She didn't like the flash and wondered if there was something better. She'd search, she thought, popping the flashbulb off. She realized very quickly that she didn't need the flash at all during the day. She would only need it when it was dark, but she didn't like the way it lit up the night so maybe she could find something not so obvious. She watched patiently for a while, listening to an audio book on her tape recorder. She was parked in an obscure place that was dark but she could see the entrance to the building, so she simply laid the seat back and relaxed as she listened to the story being told, only her face reaching the window. She watched them pass and then waited a few minutes before sitting up and starting her little gray, nondescript car. They obviously had all gathered for a meeting.

She followed the last Mercedes, staying two cars back. She followed them to a warehouse with big open door. Young black haired Italian boys and big black men worked on boxes carrying them into the open doors and stacking them somewhere to the left. She had been there many times with her boss. She pulled her camera and took pictures zooming in to get the perfect shot. No one paid her the least bit of attention. She started her car and left from the back exit and went to the printer shop, taking the film in and waiting for the pictures to be processed. She carried them home and placed them in a file and popped it in her drawer until she could send them to Morgan.

The next morning, she rented a big black SUV. She followed the sexy husband, this time with a different woman, getting pictures. Then she went back to Jan's penthouse, following two men who went to a house in a quiet residential area on the outskirts of downtown. She had to get into that house. She doubted that there would be a dead body in that house, but Morgan needed the pictures and any information she could find. She went back home and looked up equipment and tools for a busy PI to work with. She ordered tools to open locks and everything else she might need, then she called Maria.

She gave her the pictures and advised that this was more than enough to cream his ass in court. She agreed and Penelope went to the courthouse to file the divorce papers, setting the court hearing for as soon as possible. She didn't see Jan, but of course she didn't go near the courtrooms where he would be, if he even watched criminal proceedings anymore. As she walked down the hall, she knew that she was safe. Her career was intact and she could make a little bit of spending money even though she certainly didn't need it, but she did need to stay busy while she continued her search.

When her lock tools came in a nice little zippered leather wallet, she went back to the little house and waited for them to come out and get into the endless silver Mercedes. Evidently that was the vehicle of choice for hoods. As soon as they left, she got out of the car. The street was quiet and empty except for the occasional car driving down the narrow street. The birds chirped happily and the squirrels played. She went to the back. Even though it was quiet, she sure as hell didn't want to be seen by a nosy neighbor looking out the window. She entered a small kitchen and walked quickly from room to room. She opened a closet door and peered in. In the corner, Luke's boots that he always wore sat on the floor. They were very expensive ostrich and he was proud of them she knew. His jacket hung on the hanger. They were the only articles in the closet. She closed the door and searched the bedroom.

Off the kitchen, there was a door that led downstairs to the basement. She opened the door and peered into the darkness when she heard the garage door open and a car drive in. She ran to the kitchen door and exited, locking the cheap lock quickly. She stood in the back yard by the fence for a few minutes until she heard the front door close, and then she exited between the houses, squatting down as she passed the windows so that she wouldn't be seen. Why on earth would they come back, she asked herself? Was McNally in the basement? She got into her SUV and left. She'd change cars tomorrow. She had an appointment with one of Maria's long list of girlfriends. She thought about coming back to the house later in the day, but she didn't know if someone was sitting in the house keeping an eye on McNally, if he was still alive that is, or if they were cleaning away all traces of McNally's existence in that house if they had murdered him, but she would be there tomorrow the minute they left the house. She'd move quickly so that she'd be in and out before anyone came back to the house. She had to see what was in that basement, and she fully intended to bring her gun this time. She practiced at the gun range as often as she could and she was getting to be damned good at hitting her intended target. She wouldn't hesitate to use it either, she told herself.

She went home to wait for her appointment and when the sweet looking woman came in, she invited her to lunch because she was her usual starving self. The woman followed in her car and she led her to the hotel dining room where they drank fine wine and ate.

She wasn't as prepared as Maria, not sure if she wanted to do this. Her husband was a good man. He'd very likely come to her before long to ask her forgiveness because she knew that he loved her.

"That's fine." Penelope said. "You know what's best for you. Don't let anyone try to force you to do what they want. It's your decision and it's up to you alone to make this decision." She said, knowing Maria had forced the sweet woman to see her. "I believe that what you say is true, but if not, when you've had enough, just give me a call." She picked up her purse and handed her silver-embossed card to the woman.

The other clients, all friends of Maria's were not so forgiving. No one ever bulked at the cost of the work, happy to pay her hourly fee. It was their husband's money after all. It might as well be put it to good use. The man sure as hell didn't need it and he wasn't going to blow everything on his whore, that was for goddamned sure!

After a while, all the faces melded into one, every story exactly the same. She was sick to death of the games people played with each other. She wanted out now. Time to start accepting criminal cases, which she would be more than happy to take on as pro bono cases she thought. Those cases were likely to be a little more challenging. She looked in the yellow pages to be certain the word pro bono was in her full page ad and then waited for nightfall and the endless cheating husbands with plenty of pictures to prove it. They were all the same. These escorts sure were kept busy because as far as she could tell, there was no shortage of horny men walking around.

She saw Jan often and she became braver. He would walk down the street across from where she sat and many times would enter a department store. She'd follow discretely with nothing more than her purse on her shoulder and then buy pizza from the small kiosk near the back door that led to the busier downtown street at that entrance on the other side of the large department store. She walked amongst the busy, people-packed street to look at things, mostly shoes. She didn't have many and her tennies were no longer white, so she went shoe shopping.

Time dragged. She was sick of nasty soon to be divorcees and decided she would send them to a young attorney that she had befriended when they were students. He was young and nondescript, with the sort of looks that would not attract attention in a crowd. She took him to lunch and brought the pictures she had snapped of the cheating spouses. He was ready and hungry for the business. She handed him all the equipment she had bought that he would need to establish adultery. He was shocked and so thankful. He was young and he was easy going, not doing well as an attorney at all; the competition was just too intense for such a mild-mannered, smart but not brilliant or highly competitive young man. She showed him how to use the camera and the small tools to unlock pretty much anything; doors, cabinets, padlocks, it was all there. She talked to him about changing cars often once he started making money, what he should charge for his services, etc., trying to remember everything she could think of that would help him to get established, and then she assured him that she would send any potential work that came into her office straight to him. She gave him the information of the clients that had contacted her that week and she agreed to go with him until he felt completely comfortable on his own. She joined him a total of three times; the young man was ready and chomping at the bit to move on and be the best damned private eye/divorce attorney in the city. There would be plenty of work for him because there was no shortage of cheating spouses. Danielle was surprised and pleased to see the transformation in the quiet and oh so polite young man. He was going to be just fine she told him, and then she gave him her cell number and asked him to call her at any time even if it was late if he had any questions at all or if he needed help. She gave him her course books to be licensed as a private investigator and he was ready in less than a week. He passed the course with flying colors and hung out his shingle over the door of his small, one room storefront he had rented and converted into a cozy PI/divorce attorney's office and the work came in fast and hard. He called once to talk to her about disguises and that was pretty much the last time she talked to him, even though he loved Danielle with all his heart and he always had. Life was just too damned busy now for any kind of relationship, and he knew he had as much chance with her as an ice cube in hell anyway.

The next morning she drove back to the safe house. It sat on a quiet tree lined street, evidently every one gone to work on this Wednesday morning. This time she was in a small Honda. She parked across the street back from the house and waited for the Mercedes to pass. She got out and entered through the back door and went directly to the basement, flipping on the light switch but leaving the door open for a quick getaway. There was a cot with a pillow and a blanket. On the far wall there were two chains with metal rings that would clasp the wrists. Where was Luke? Did they have him? She hadn't seen him in the car when they passed, but she hadn't been looking either. Maybe they took him to the warehouse, and he was somewhere in a back room. She'd never know. There were men there 24/7. Drugs were a booming business and holding a kidnap victim at the warehouse hardly seemed like something Jan might do, although she couldn't imagine why. It would be easier to just kill him and dump the body where it would never be found. It just didn't make any sense. Seeing his clothes had given her hope but he was very likely dead and buried in some remote place, but still....she hoped.

She went upstairs and checked the closet again. Nothing had changed and then she left, taking his boots and his coat with her. He would be very happy when he had his boots back on his feet. She locked the door and drove away.

She went to lunch and watched for Jan and then went home. The flowering trees had been planted and were doing quite well, at least for now. Her home/office was so pretty with the long narrow porch and the flowering baskets that ran the full length of her porch and the little yard with the emerald grass and quaint walk that led to the porch. She walked the neighborhood, wanting to know every nook and cranny for an escape route. She didn't know why, but she felt that it was important to be ready for anything. And the work came in. There were plenty of drunken drivers who got caught driving while they were either high or drunk or both, but she sent them to another friend that she had gone to school with who specialized in such things. She waited for something juicier that could sink her teeth into.

In the meantime, she'd search for Luke. He was alive; she just knew it and she knew that she would find him. Oh yes, she would find him very soon now and she would bring him home. She continued to follow Jan and then his buddies, but it led to nothing of importance as far as she could tell.

She went back to the car rental and rented a lime green Volkswagen. They knew she was a PI and they expected her every few days. She loved that little car; she could whip through the streets of Savannah with ease.

She pulled into the Volkswagen dealer a few days later and bought her own lime green baby. Then she went to the busy drug warehouse, she parked in front and went in. She looked cute as hell, her cleavage falling out of the bodice of her dress, her makeup so lovely and her lips so red. She was ready for the boys.

"Hi. She said to the heavy weight Italian man. She vaguely recognized him, but she knew the mean-looking gangster didn't have a clue who she was.

"Hey Lady, turn around and get your ass back to your green car. I don't want you here." He said gruffly, a cigar clamped between his teeth and he turned away writing on a tablet held firmly on his clipboard, watching his men and shouting orders.

"Oh, okay I'm leaving right now. I'm just looking for my boyfriend. He hasn't returned any of my calls."

"Geraldo, help the lady and then escort her to her car. Don't come back here again, Lady. If your boyfriend does work here, he sure won't have a job much longer." And he turned away to answer the phone that rang insistently in the office.

"What's your boyfriend's name, pretty lady?" He asked as the men continued to work, ignoring them. This was good, she thought.

"Roman Russo." She lied, looking into his very handsome face. Were there really that many good-looking men or was she just not the particular, she wondered.

"Never heard of him, Angel."

"That fucker!" She exploded. "I knew it. The cheating lying son-of-a-bitch is with that whore, Margo! Well she can have him, I'm done." She said looking through the open doors of the warehouse as well as any undercover could. She took in everything. Then she headed for her car; just not that much to see really and she was pretty certain McNally wouldn't be brought to this place anyway.

"Hey, I'm here for you anytime you're ready for a real man. Just come by and let me take you to dinner." He said, looking her up and down appreciatively.

"Really? You married?" She asked suspiciously as he followed to the open door.

"Who cares? She's always sleeping." He said, leaning against her little car. "Man's got to relief himself somehow and the hand just ain't enough anymore.

She opened her car door and leaned in the open window before getting into the driver's seat. "Tell me about it. I have the same problem."

"Well, I can certainly help you with your problem, little lady. Give me a kiss, you sweet angel." He said, grabbing her arm and pulling her against him. She giggled and cuddled up to his chest, rubbing it with her little white hands. His erection was quite visible. What the hell. Did no one have a tiny dick anymore?

He kissed her and then tried to pull her dress off her shoulders, but she pushed the horny idiot away. Oh yeah, she was definitely going to be back for this one.

"When do you get off work?" She asked.

'Every afternoon at exactly 6 p.m." He said.

"Friday good?" She asked, getting in the driver's seat and starting the little car.

"Friday's perfect. My little fat Bonita goes out with the girls on Fridays."

"Okay. Meet me at the hotel where I stay and I'll show you a really good time, Geraldo." She gave him the name of the hotel and said, "See ya." And she meant it. With time, he was going to let her into the warehouse. She was fairly sure that Luke wasn't there, but she wanted to be 100% certain and not leave any rock unturned. This was just too important to skip any steps.

She went to the hotel and got a suite for Friday night. She wanted someplace big and nice where they could be comfortable and just cozy up together. She wanted to get to know him, but even more than that, she wanted in that warehouse. She ordered many bottles of champagne and fine bourbon, and then went into the dining room. She chose a dark table and ordered a small prime rib. It was early, not yet 4:00, but she certainly wouldn't want anything else for the rest of the day, except wine of course. The coffee was the best she had ever tasted and she would likely drink many cups of the stuff when she finished her meal. As she waited for her food, she drank her one glass of wine, and there was Jan, as big as day and just as handsome. He was sitting at a very small round table near the middle of the room. He had a woman and he was holding her hand across the small table as he talked to her. She wasn't really very attractive, but she looked intelligent and terribly bored. She watched them as she ate. He didn't even glance her way. This was good, she thought, but she was quite thankful for her disguise.

She drank and smoked, reading the murder mystery that she had just bought, sliding around the small rounded seat of her booth until she faced way from Jan and his female companion. He didn't look, but she sure as hell wasn't taking any chances. She thought about following them, but really? They were probably going right upstairs to have what looked like it might some very boring sex, probably not though. She didn't look like the sort of woman who would enjoy an afternoon quickie. She drank and smoked and read and then left.

She got wine and her cigarettes and turned on TV to a stupid sitcom. She liked the noise. She drank and smoked, took a shower and hit the hay. Morning came early and there was so much to do, thinking about the penthouse. She'd go to the penthouse garage tomorrow and she'd have to change vehicles very soon, she thought as she drifted into sleep.

In the morning, she listened to her messages. The woman left her name and number and disconnected. She called her back and asked her what she could do for her.

"You're pro bono, right?"

"Yes, I am, at least for a few cases."

"Even if it's a murder case?"

"Especially if it's a murder case."

"So you are experienced then?" She asked suspiciously, sounding **exhausted.**

"Yes ma'am." She lied. "You're exhausted aren't you?" And the woman began to cry for her young son. He didn't do it. His friend did.

"Would you like to come to my office in the morning?" She asked, writing down the woman's name.

"No. The hurricane is supposed to hit tonight, and I don't want to be swimming for my life."

"Okay." She said. "Just call me when you're ready."

She had no idea that there was hurricane headed straight for Savannah from the Atlantic. She never watched the weather channel or even the news anymore. But it was definitely raining cats and dogs as she opened the door and stood under the covered porch, looking out at the pounding rain. She sure as hell wouldn't need to water this week, she thought, hoping her young trees would survive. She set the security alarm and went to her office/bedroom, poured champagne and flipped on the news. The weather guy was damned excited and she watched for the rest of the day as they tracked the storm with radar. Good, she thought, I can sleep all day. I'm certainly going to need my energy for Friday night. She knew a hurricane would never stop her sexy companion. He was going to get laid if he had anything to say about it….and so was she. It had been far too long for this little girl. She hoped her wig stayed on. She'd be sure to secure it with 100 clips. Then she fell asleep.

The hurricane woke her at 3:00 a.m. She got up and walked to the porch and then into the parking lot, not the least bit intimated by the wind that tried to lift her light body and carry her away. It was exhilarating; she thought happily as she lifted her arms and twirled. When she got back to the office, her gown and her hair were dripping wet, making a big puddle as she walked. She jumped into a warm shower, washing her hair and then her wig and placing it back on the wig stand to dry. She sat down and shaved the tender skin of her vagina. There was no way Geraldo would believe that she was a true blond if she had thick Mexican pubic hairs, and for some reason unknown to her, it seemed important that he not know. She never even allowed stumble to form anymore. She loved her smooth vagina, putting thick lotion on the tender skin daily to prevent a rash. It had stung for a few days at first, but not anymore, thank God. Then she put on winter pajamas and grabbed another bottle of champagne to wait out the lovely storm. Eventually she would throw the wig away but maybe she'd keep the blue contacts. She loved their color.

She got wine and her cigarettes and turned on TV to yet another stupid sitcom because she liked the noise. She drank one glass of champagne and smoked one cigarette and then went back to sleep. Morning was really going to feel like it came early for sure and there was so much to do, thinking about the penthouse. She'd go to the parking structure again tomorrow; she'd have to change vehicles very soon, she thought as she drifted into sleep, but her little green car was always there parked in the little parking lot, waiting for her with a happy lime green grin. Her name was Little Limon, lime in Mexican.

She met her hot Italian the next evening. He had never been to the hotel before and when they were seated, he looked around curiously.

"This looks expensive." He said picking up the menu.

"So the fuck what?" She said exasperated. If he wanted to get laid, he'd better just shut up, or she'd march right back out the door. "You're turning me off boy."

He laughed and they ate and went up to the hotel suite. "Goddamn girl! Can I be your boyfriend, he said as she gave him the expensive whiskey. They sat on the couch and turned on the news. Another hurricane on its way. Yaaa Hoo.

"Man I love, love, love this weather." She told him.

"Really, my wife hates it. She always tries to keep me home."

"Why do you stay married? You said yourself she was fat and dumpy."

"Yeah, she really is. The cellulite is a little hard to look at but she's warm."

"You have kids?"

"Not from her." Was all he said.

She didn't really give a shit. Just making that ole conversation. After they had finished eating and went to the suite, they just drank and talked like old buddies, getting absolutely snockered. When they finally crawled into the big bed, they fell unconscious, both drunk as skunks. He snored just like Luke. The thought made her sad and restless as she remembered his snoring from the couch in his office. She rolled over and went back to sleep. She woke in the morning to the flushing of the toilet. He came out and she got up and walked to the couch, the fireplace blazed happily and the wind howled, shaking the windows.

"Hey Baby. Sorry we got so snockered last night. That certainly wasn't my plan."

"God, don't worry about it little one. The bed was heavenly."

"Want to eat here or go downstairs?"

"Downstairs would be great. I'm paying this time."

"No you aren't. I have more money than I'll ever be able to spend in this lifetime."

"You have sugar daddies?"

"Yes sir, more than one." She lied.

"Dang. Let's get married."

Mr. Jan Anderson wouldn't like that."

"Whose he?"

"You're boss."

"You mean that old gray haired guy? Can he even get it up?"

"You have no idea. That old man curl's these little toes with utter, unbridled joy. He makes me moan with unbridled passion." And she realized all of a sudden that she really, really missed that man.

"Wow. Have you seen his fat wife? His daughters are kind of cute, a little too young to do anyone any good for now though."

She laughed and they went to breakfast.

"Tell me all about your job. You sure have a lot of boxes lying around that big warehouse. What on earth is in them?"

"Not sure." He lied. "We're told to count and we do... all day long. And then we stack. I think its coffee. At least it smells like coffee."

"My poor dumb big hunk. Come on. You're Italian. You know very well what's in all those boxes."

"Yeah, plenty of cocaine and tar heroin, at least I think that might be it. No pills though, as far as I know, but maybe. We sure don't ever look inside. The men come every night and cart most of the product away. The drug kings have got to have one hell of a distribution center, that's for sure, but it's not anything we should be talking about. I could lose more than just my job if anyone knew I was discussing this with you."

"I've asked Jan to take me there, but he always declines. He wants me to learn his businesses, but evidently not that one." She told him truthfully." He lets me take care of all his real estate and his illegal offshore accounts. I love it, but it is a little boring. If it wasn't for the sex, I'd be out of there." She lied as she ate and drank the hot coffee. "Do you think we'll ever be lovers, my friend?"

"Sure if you want to. I've been waiting to go back up that elevator."

"I don't want to Geraldo. I need a friend more than I need a lover." She said taking his hand and kissing the palm. "Can we do that?"

"I would love to be your friend, Penelope Scott. I can't think of anything that would be more fun."

"Okay, my new bestest friend." She said offering her hand across the table to shake.

"What do you do for fun, friend?"

"Anything you want. I'm buying a boat soon."

"Really? Ocean going?"

"Of course. Let's run away. Can you scuba dive?"

"Are you kidding? My wife would never agree to that one?"

"God Geraldo. Why in the hell would any man who looks like you put up with that?"

"I'm at a loss to explain."

"Let's learn together."

"Where?"

"I'll let you know. Do you have a gun?"

"Nope. Had to get rid of it a long time ago. Threw it in the river."

"Let's go this weekend and make you a legal gun owner, then we can learn to shoot together at the indoor range."

"You're fun, Penelope."

"Yes. I am. And rich to boot."

They went home to wait for the weekend. When she walked in the phone was ringing. It was the sad woman, sounding much better. They made an appointment for an hour and she went to take a shower. The woman and her 13 year old son arrived right on time and she took them to the couch.

"My goodness, this is absolutely gorgeous."

Penelope led them to the kitchen first and she got Eric a Pepsi and then to her huge bathroom. She liked to hear the woman ooh and aah. Then they went to the front office desk and sat down. She turned on the recorder and waited. She told her about the party and how it had gotten out of hand. His friend had taken the gun from him and was shooting it off in the living room. He and a couple of friends told the cops that her son had been the one to shoot the girl and they did lift his finger prints from the gun along with the other boy who Eric claimed fired the gun into the room. It was his father's and he stole it from his father's old cabinet where it had been locked securely for years. She worked nights and had no idea what her son was up to.

She turned to the young boy and began to ask him questions, which he answered clearly and without hesitation. He took the gun only to show off in front of his friends, the ones who were always calling him momma's good little boy. She knew the kid was telling the truth. He was out on bail and the court date was set for two months from today.

"This is going to be cake. I don't want either of you to worry. Eric, go to school and come straight home every single day. Do not under any circumstances discuss any of this with anyone but your mother or me."

"Yes ma'am, I sure will."

"Okay. If either of you have any questions call me immediately, and she gave them each a card with her phone number embossed in silver and they left. She went to the police department and talked to the arresting officer. He told her that he was pretty certain that the young skinny kid wasn't the villain here, but he had to take him in.

"Did the other boys walk?"

"Yep. Right out the door into the yard."

"Okay, I'll see you in court Officer Maloney, she said, shaking his hand.

"I'll be there beautiful lady. You can bet on it." And she left. She was worried that Jan would be there, but he wasn't. Of course she didn't look back once, but there was no way to disguise her voice. Oh well what would be would be. She wasn't going to work much longer anyway. She and Eric took their places as the judge entered and the bailiff announced him. She knew him. He had once been an acquaintance whom she had exchanged pleasantries with, but he obviously didn't recognize her and that strengthened her confidence that she could move about the courthouse and not be recognized.

She called Officer Maloney to the stand and he walked the court through the crime scene. He was an excellent witness, sometimes looking at the jury to drive home a point. Neither of the other boys was in the courtroom because she did not subpoena them. He told them that he doubted that Eric Halsted was the shooter. The only crime he had committed was that he had brought a loaded gun to the party, for which he would do community work until his crime was paid in full. But of course, nothing could bring Melissa Rodriquez back. Her parents sat in the courtroom and the woman cried softly as her husband held her. Then it was over. Eric Halsted was found not guilty of all charges. His mother was bouncing off the ceiling with joy. The boy simply looked relieved. She took them across the street for lunch and they left.

Penelope went home and filed the folder. That was it. No more. Then she called Geraldo. He had passed security and they could pick up his gun. They met every afternoon to shoot. The new boat was tied up on the dock just waiting for the weekend. She met him at the scuba diving pool and they began. It didn't take long and they were in the ocean. Drifting happily together as the tanks bubbled. She had plans for him. He was going to let her into the warehouse. All she had to do was wait for the shift change.

They traveled on the weekends as much as his work and his commitment to his wife would allow, never going too far from home, looking for reefs with lots of fishes and clear blue waters. With time, when they had finished diving, they would climb into the boat and she began to slowly seduce him, wanting to make him want her more than he had ever wanted anyone. And he did. He was a fantastic lover and he was so much fun too. She hated to say good-bye but she knew it was coming to end now.

She finally met him at the warehouse and he let her in. As he worked, she explored. No one paid the least bit of attention to her. It was the middle of the night and there was much to do. She found a door at the end of the warehouse and around the corner. McNally's room. She could smell his very distinctive body odor when he hadn't had a bath for a while. How long had they held him there she wondered. It didn't make any sense. Why would they drag him from one place to another? Why hadn't Jan just had him killed? She didn't have the answers. She was going to find her darling very horny boss if it was the last thing she ever did. He wasn't far and she knew she would be bringing him home soon.

The next morning she went back to the house and looked in the basement. Nothing had changed. It was time to follow some gangsters, which she did the next morning, driving far behind. Her little green Limon was very noticeable; so she'd get a Mercedes today. She was very likely going to have to lease one for a while because she thought that few car rentals carried such luxuries as far as she knew, but she was able to find a car rental that did rent Mercedes, a blue sports car that Mercedes had just put on the market. She would keep it for as long as she could.

She went home and transcribed the Halsted tape. She filed it and poured alcohol. She lit a cigarette and went outside, sitting in the long wooden swing on the porch. The wooden swing that hung from heavy chains looked quite nice sitting at the end of her long narrow porch, she thought. She was tired. Another storm was building and the sky was almost black. Just tropical this time.

She followed the first gangsters she saw staying behind, but not so far this time. Mercedes were everywhere, most of them gray. They led her to a different house this time. She had been there one time to interview a client who was in hiding. It was a safe house that was very well protected for the young idiots who had been arrested. Jan had told her that it was a safe house for those escaping justice before fleeing to Mexico or Portugal. She knew instinctively that McNally was there. If he wasn't, no one would bother with the house, only when there were prisoners or people in wait, which of course could be possible so she'd have to be very careful because there would be a gangster keeping watch over the person hiding there. What the fuck was Jan thinking? It just didn't make any sense. He still had McNally even though she certainly was no threat to him now. Ohhhhhh, okay! He knew that she loved McNally. Of course they had listened in to their conversation and were watching when she would sit on his lap and kiss him passionately. That was it, she knew now why Jan had done this and it made her angry enough to want to stab the petty little crime boss in the heart. It was so senseless to imprison a man for almost two years for nothing more than jealousy. Jan had a serious personality defect she realized as she drove toward the office. Why he hadn't killed him was still a mystery to her. He certainly wasn't holding him for ransom.

She went home and showered, taking off her wig and placing it on the dummy head. She towel dried her hair and dressed in one of the sexiest dresses she owned. She put on her thin strapped sandals with small blue rhinestones and then sprayed her face with the ivory foundation to perfection and then she put on her all-day-long lipstick and drove to the penthouse. In the elevator, she punched the penthouse and called Geraldo. Telling him that she was with her Jan and she needed him to stay on the line. She instructed him to call the police if she screamed and gave him the address, talking to him pleasantly as she walked through the open door and sat at Jan's desk.

"You trying to get me killed Penelope?" He asked, truly alarmed.

Jan said nothing as he listened to her phone call. She needed a witness if he tried to have her taken away, not sure that he would even give enough of a shit to bother now. What reason could he possibly have at this point;

none at all. She certainly was no threat to him and very likely never had been. She hung up as he sat a glass of champagne and bourbon down on the desk. He took a drink and watched her, pulling a cigar from the expensive humidor and cutting it. He clamped it in his mouth and leaned back, waiting. Just like her McNally, she thought.

"Delicious." She said, drinking the too expensive for anybody but the very rich champagne. "I've missed you Jan. All I can think of lately is how you made me writhe with unadulterated pleasure."

"There's the couch, my lovely whore. You've cut your hair."

"Yes. Too thick, too long. It was time. Who knew it was curly."

"Why are you here?"

"I want to take you to lunch."

"Okay." He said getting up and heading for the door his body lean and muscled, his ass tight.

He was so handsome to her still. She hoped he would make her writhe again.

She led him to her rented blue Mercedes and drove. He gave her the directions to a restaurant by the sea that he wanted to try.

"How are Celeste and the girls?"

"Winning ribbons like crazy."

"Good for them."

"You're beautiful. I hope you don't ever change your hair."

"I sure won't. That's a promise I'll keep."

"Good."

She took the long drive to the front of the white plantation building and handed the maître d the keys. They drank in the lovely restaurant and ate delicious food, but just like every man she had ever known, she thought all food was just amazing. She had dessert and then coffee.

"There's a hotel upstairs."

"Yes."

"Can I entice you in a little afternoon delight?" She asked, her voice husky with desire, remembering.

He took her up to a suite on the 3rd floor and held the door for her as she walked in.

"Lovely." She said. Then they sat on the couch.

He ordered room service and the bucket with bottles of champagne was delivered. "You remembered."

"Of course. Take off your clothes, but leave those shoes on and then walk to me." She did, so turned on she could hardly contain herself. She stood in front of him as he watched her silently, drinking his whiskey. Then she went back to couch and pulled her legs under her. She could wait. She had all day with nothing to do but find out where her old boss was being held.

"You've gotten some sun." He said watching her firm ass as she moved to the couch and took a drink of champagne.

"Are still mad at me?"

"Of course not. I moved the money as soon as I went back to the office from our lunch date. Everything tucked away safe and sound. They tried to arrest me, but it lasted about 35 minutes and I was back at my desk."

"Oh thank God." She said, truly relieved. "There can be nothing worse than the hot and vicious vengeance of a woman scorned."

"I understood. You were trying to protect your lover. Did you ever find him?"

"No, I did not, and McNally was never my lover, Jan. He obviously died somewhere. I of course have not heard a word from him in years. He's gone now and I've finally had to come to grips with that and moved on with my life. I bought a boat and I spend a lot of time out on the ocean. Not far. I like to explore the reefs if they aren't too far out."

"You dive?"

"Yes. I do."

"By yourself?"

"Yes. Just me and the deep blue sea." She lied.

He got up and came to sit by her, looking at her bare vagina. "I like that. Nothing like a sweet vagina to turn any man on earth on." He said rubbing it and inserting his middle finger into the warm wetness. Then he took of a sip of the alcohol, looking straight ahead. She could wait. She liked the suspense.

"It's going to storm again. Quite a year."

"Yes, but it's just an unnamed tropical storm this time."

"Did you like DC?" Looking into her lovely dark eyes for a reaction.

"Of course not. Someone tried to mug and blackened my eye so bad I couldn't see out of it for days. I couldn't get out of there fast enough and get back to the safety of Savannah." And she knew without a doubt who had hired that someone.

"I had no idea you were back." Yeah fucker, I know, she thought, getting angry.

He watched the news and she drank and smoked. She got up and flipped on the fireplace and opened the linen closet for a pillow and light blanket as he admired those nice white breasts with the pink nipples. He was glad she was back he thought as she laid her head on the pillow. He watched the news and she drifted into sleep, quite tipsy now, lulled by the rain and wind outside the windows. He watched her as she slept. Then he pulled the blanket and he laid his head on her stomach, and then down, sniffing her sweet smelling pussy. He sat up and finished his drink, pouring another and watching the news. The weather was nonstop.

With time he spread her silky thighs and moved to her bare vagina, inserting his finger in her and licking gently with his tongue, like a cat's, she thought. She woke and grabbed the sides of his face, but lay still just enjoying the sensation as his rough tongue licked and sucked gently. When she began to moan just like the Mexican slut that she was, he couldn't wait any longer. Her smooth vagina was waiting for him. He sometimes thought about having sex with a young inexperienced girl for some reason, but of course he never would even think of such a terrible act; he had 2 little girls of his own that he would protect with this life. He entered her roughly, ramming just the way she always liked it, staring at her wet red lips. She moaned, clutching him, but he continued to ride up and down. He shuttered and fell on her, his face in her neck, trying to catch his breath. She held onto him until he moved to a sitting position, zipping back up his very expensive suit pants. As usual he didn't strip, simply pulling it from its nest. He probably felt too vulnerable without his pants, she thought.

His unattractive and somber attorney now just wasn't the woman that this one was. She was in her 30s and cold as a stone. She had never climaxed even though he felt honor bound to make that happen for her, but she never did, just too cold, too uninterested, having sex simply to keep her job or move up the corporate ladder maybe. He didn't know and he sure as hell didn't care. With time he left her alone to her duties, but he watched her like a hawk, ready to make a move the minute anything looked suspicious, tracking everything she did through the dedicated office manager who kept track of every piece of paper she touched. He had learned his lesson.

He pulled his cell phone and called his wife; he wouldn't be home tonight so please don't wait up. He knew she knew. His Celeste had been told by many of his

women, always so vindictive. He hated that they made
her cry, but he would hold her gently and she would smile
again. He poured them both another drink, lighting
his cold cigar, getting up to empty ashtray. His shirt
and pants were wrinkle free, she thought lazily. They
always were. They watched the news, smoked and drank
just like old times. He rubbed her small feet lazily as
he watched. She loved him again, and told him so. He
said nothing. Things were back to normal, so glad that
Giovanni hadn't succeeded. He smiled remembering at
the man's total humiliation. He had run into a wild cat
that time, totally unexpected. His balls had been swollen
terribly for days according to the men who watched him
hobble around the city, getting a big kick out of his pain
at the hands of the fiery little Mexican.

She slept again, waking up to his tongue and his
relentless pounding. She got up and took a shower. He
had always loved the way she kept herself. She never wore
perfume at his request; but she always smelled like lemon
blossoms. He loved that about her.

She took him back to the penthouse and he exited
the car, not saying good-bye. Everything was back to
normal. He had asked her if she was still an attorney and
she simply said no, adding that McNally had left millions
at her disposal.

"Good for you. Spend it while you can."

The last thing she needed was for this man to start
watching her again. He didn't ask her where she was

staying, but that certainly didn't matter. If he wanted to know, he would. She had an important job to do and this man would never be allowed to interfere. If he tried to come after her or McNally again, she would shoot him dead on the street as he walked past her and then disappear into the crowd. No one would ever know, especially if she wore her disguise.

She went to bed early because it was going to be a busy morning. McNally waited. She knew it, she just knew. Call it woman's intuition. She drove directly to the safe house and went to the back door, breaking one of the glass panes and unlocking the door. There was no vehicle outside or in the small garage as far as she could tell and she made the decision to move forward, her gun in her pocket and loaded. He was in the first bedroom aslecp, tied to the bed with a rope. She pulled her knife and began to saw on the rope, waking him with a jerk, his eyes filled with fear and confusion, not knowing what was happening. He looked at her, confused. What on earth was this woman doing sawing at his ropes? She went to kitchen and found vegetable scissors and came back. She cut the rope and told him to get up now. The fun times were over and work called.

"Danielle?" He asked stunned.

"Yeah, let's go McNally."

They left from the front door, leaving it open and walked to the blue Mercedes. She drove them straight to the office.

"What the fuck have you done, you stupid cunt. I'm not living here! You ruined it!" He exploded, looking at his now white building and all the flowers. God, she even made a yard, taking up his parking for his customers; customers who only came one at a time, leaving a huge asphalt area for just him and his stupid Mercedes.

"You're right, you're not living here. This is my house now. You got your money. Go buy yourself your own fucking house why don't you, you cheap son-of-a-bitch."

She opened the door and walked in tossing her purse on the desk, slamming the damned door behind her. Nothing ever changed with this half-wit.

"What the fuck! You've ruined this place. My pride and joy!!" He shouted, truly broken hearted. She watched him and sneered, wishing she had locked the fucking door behind her when she came in.

"Yeah. I should have left you to rot asshole."

Not a thing had changed and she quickly began to regret finding him and rescuing the stupid man. Why in the hell did she do that? Her life was so much more pleasant without this stupid jerk in it; he caused her nothing but grief and irritation. How in the hell could she have forgotten that, she asked herself as she watched him looking around in sheer horror. Asshole!

He went into the office, keeping his mouth shut and sat on the couch watching the news from the huge screen.

"At least you did something right," he said pointing at the big screen up on the wall.

"Glad you like it."

"Where's my cigars?"

"Right where you left them. Just look around." She said, not bothering to point out the sophisticated humidor that he bought years ago and filled with the best cigars he could find this side of Cuba.

He found them. Still fresh, he thought, quite amazed. It had been years since he had smoked one of these babies. He prepared it and lit it. Wow, his expensive cigar lighter still worked too he said, laying his head back on the couch and blowing smoke toward the ceiling in sheer heaven.

She got up and poured him a Chivas Regal. She wasn't drinking today. She was hungry and wanted to go eat. They went downtown to his favorite café. It was crowded, just about every table filled; no one sure as hell was going to eat outside today. Hurricane season would be over soon and the sun would come out, he told her. He ate like a starving man. When they had finished she took him to the hotel and went into her hotel suite, handing him the key card. Then she handed him the bank card. He sat on the couch and she asked him if he wanted a drink.

"No. I just want to watch the news and go to sleep. Those fucking iron beds with the thin mattresses were miserable." She got up and sat on his lap, leaning her head back on his arm.

"I'm ashamed to admit how many tears I shed for you. I was desperate to find you."

He pulled her up and kissed her beautiful red lips. Lemon flowers. Some things never changed. He held her and watched the news. She fell asleep on the long couch, but he stayed awake all night watching the news and drinking the whiskey like a starving man.

Her work was done and she had a murder mystery to read. She drove back to the office and called the car rental to come and pick up the little Mercedes while McNally snored. She got some white wine and a cigarette and threw a pillow on the couch, lying back to read. She called Morgan with the news telling him about her long hunt and how she found him.

"Congratulations. I mean it, Danielle. You are just amazing. If you are ever looking for employment, please call me first.

"It's tempting Morgan, but then I'd have to live in Washington, DC. I just couldn't do it. Six months was more than enough for this woman."

"I promise you, you get used to it."

"Nope, but love you, mean it."

The phone rang and she got up and sat at the desk and answered it. It had to be McNally but how did he even get this number? He must have looked in the yellow pages or called the operator with just his address.

"Did you ever finish the Massey case?"

"No. Their father was dead and they decided to just leave it alone. They decided that the Mafia was just no one to mess with."

"Okay. See ya. Let's go to dinner tonight." He said. "Then I'm going to fuck your brains out, since I happen to be paying out a fortune to keep you in style. Do I even have any money left?" He asked.

"That's a deal." She said, ignoring his question. Some things just never changed, and fortunately, his dick had been too limp for too long now, thank God. The poor thing couldn't possibly have anything more than a distant memory of an erection anymore.

The car rental company came and picked up the little blue Mercedes, which she certainly didn't need anymore. She waited until 6:00. McNally had no coat and she pulled his big feather down coat from the closet. He hated to be babied, but that was tough shit. He'd need it. An ice storm was on its way and the last thing this very thin, obviously severely mal-nourished man needed right now was pneumonia; it could easily take his life and she had no intensions of having to bury the man anytime soon.

When she knew she had found him, she had gone to the Justin Boot Fair and bought his favorite ostrich boots. The others she took from the closet were old and the skin had dried out and left nasty looking bare spots. He wore a 13, but she had no trouble finding a pair. McNally had big hands, big feet, and a little dick as far as she knew. If that wasn't true, he would have been pulling it out to show his very young secretary proudly, but he almost never did do that. She then bought him three pair of blue jeans and boxer shorts and polo shirts of every color. Then some suits and white shirts and ties, his work apparel. She put them in the trunk and carried them to the hotel room. He looked in the bag and pulled the boots. He picked her up and swung her around, dropping her on the couch. Then he took his clothes and ran to the big shower. He hadn't had a shower in years, and he showered twice a day now, but with time, he had no longer smelled like BO, at least as far as he could smell. He washed happily, singing at the top of his lungs as he poured a huge amount of the sudsy foam onto the wash cloth. He got out, shaved and splashed the good smelling shaving lotion on his face and got dressed. This was a damned handsome man in a polo shirt and blue jeans, but he was so thin, he looked almost skeletal, the bones in his face prominent, she thought. She didn't like it; he just wasn't her big muscular McNally anymore. But it wouldn't be long before he'd be back to his old self. The man ate constantly and she planned to encourage that for a while.

"Let's go, my future bride. I'm not going to let you out of my sight after this. What a woman. I mean it Danielle. I am one fucking lucky son-of-a-bitch."

"I know that you're saying these things because you're thrilled to be wearing those damned ugly boots again, but I must say that it is certainly about time you finally figured out for yourself just how much you need me, Mr. Attorney and all on your own too. I'm impressed." She said as she followed him out the door.

They had to walk to the steak house that he was dying to get back to because they cooked his porter house steaks to perfection, but he refused to get into her Little Limon, even after she told him she would leave his ass there if he didn't get in the car. Steak called to him, but he'd starve before he got into anything so small and girlie. It was just a tin can and they wouldn't live through an accident, he told her. Slob. He hadn't changed a bit! They ate and then ordered liquor. Why she didn't even think to simply drive to the restaurant and leave the son-of-a-bitch to get there as best he could was beyond her, but it was definitely nice to finally be getting some much needed exercise; it felt so good to be moving her body again.

"What the hell happened to my brand new Mercedes?" He asked, eyeing her suspiciously.

"Beats me. You snooze you lose. It was probably stolen months ago." What a fucking idiot. It was right there in the parking lot. The man was losing his ability to focus for sure.

"This is just like old times Danielle. I prayed that you would find me and I knew that you would look for me; at least I prayed that you would. I swear to God, I knew. I'm not kidding when I tell you that we're going to be married." He informed her.

"Great McNally. Buy a house, buy the most expensive diamond set you can find. On second thought, let me buy it."

"Okay. I can't stand being in that fucking office for one more second." He lied. He loved the lawn. He loved the porch with all the beautiful flowering baskets. She knew he was lying; the man could never fool her for one second. You'd think he'd have learned that by now.

"You haven't seen the new kitchen yet and I don't think you went into the lovely new bathroom, either McNally." He had not, just going to the parking lot and letting it hang out in the wind. So much better than the can he had been forced to use during his captivity, unless someone came in and let him use the bathroom, which wasn't often enough.

"That place is so much more than you deserve McNally, but it's mine now, so don't even worry about it. And you've lost weight. Didn't they ever feed you?"

"No. Sometimes someone would throw me a candy bar and a burrito or taco. Most times I got nothing. I don't think they were intentionally trying to starve me to death; they simply didn't remember that I needed to eat, like maybe one guy thought the other guy was bringing me food or something. God, who even knows the thoughts of stupid men who had no woman in their face to remind them that food is a necessity to living."

"Sweet Jesus, how on earth did you stay busy?"

"I thought about you. I knew you'd come and I was happy to wait. I'm going to marry you Danielle."

"Will you work?"

"Of course. We'll have a hell of a business together."

She left him at the hotel and drove home. He called her and said he had made an appointment with the real estate agent in the hotel, surprising her beyond words. She parked on the street and met him in the bar. They went to the woman, and followed her to an extremely nice suburb. "Wow McNally I'm impressed."

"I've always had good taste, Danielle." He assured her.

"Really? I sure would not know a thing about that; although I do admit that desk of yours is exquisite."

"You know that I want something with land and she says she has the perfect house for me…for us." Another shocker.

They looked at 4 homes, each one with a circular drive and an electronic gate that let them in and kept the unwanted guests out, but that wasn't what either of them wanted. He wanted acreage and he was determined to have it. She finally took them to a big white house that sat way back off the lovely lane that ran past the property, and there was more acreage that came with the house than he had hoped for, so they both felt it was the perfect place for them. She wanted a pool and he agreed to have one put in as soon as the ground warmed up enough to dig. He told the realtor to meet them in a few days to draw up the contract.

"You're paying cash, McNally." She informed him.

"Now why the hell would I do that, Herrera? I've got to build me some credit."

"Oh bullshit." She said, turning to the happy agent. "I guarantee he will write a check. I've got the check book."

And they left. They signed the papers the next afternoon and she handed him the check book. He wrote it for the full asking price without complaint. They left and went to the department store, heading immediately to the pizza kiosk. She knew he hadn't tasted pizza for years. Actually, she never remembered him eating pizza. He devoured a half pizza and drank a huge soda happily. Then he dragged her to the jewelry department.

"What the hell McNally, you can't be serious."

"Oh but I'm very serious."

"Okay McNally. When you come to your senses, I'll give it back to you, receipt and all.

"Marrying you is all I thought about for two years. I want babies."

"You are a fucking liar, McNally." But she chose a beautiful diamond studded platinum band, tiny diamonds covering the whole ring."

She put it on and then told him that they could walk back to the office and she would drive him back to the hotel but he refused and called a cab. She was truly getting so sick of his ridiculous attitude so she simply left him there and walked away without even a good-bye to the idiot. When he came to the office the next day by cab, she made him sit at the computer and look at furniture. Surprisingly, he had exquisite taste, and he bought everything immediately.

"Do you have the address?"

"No where's the contract?"

"Okay. No problem." she said, picking up the phone. She dialed the real estate office and asked for Judy and wrote down the address for him.

"Where are the keys to your Mercedes, McNally?"

"I honestly don't know what happened to them."

"Okay, I'm going to call someone who can replace the ignition so that you'll have a new key. The mechanic will likely have tools to get the door unlocked so that you can finally have your stupid manly man's car back; it couldn't have more than 100 miles on it McNally because you went missing right after you told me you were going to buy a new car."

"Good idea. I'm going call to my mechanic and have it towed there right now." He said, pulling his new cell phone from his shirt pocket. In the meantime, he had rented a shiny black SUV which he really liked, maybe better than the sedan he had been so proud of. He thought he would sell the Mercedes and buy an SUV. She followed him to the beach where they ate breakfast; he still refused to bless her Little Limon with his useless bony ass, which was fine and dandy with her. He was nothing more than a Neanderthal wearing modern day clothes and he had about as much sense when it came to women as far as she could tell. After they ate, they went their separate ways. She read and slept as the rain pounded.

She didn't see him for weeks after that which was just fine with her.

But he did come to the office to tell her about the furniture and how lovely the house was. Time to get the business rolling, he said. She took notes as he talked. Danielle McNally and Luke McNally, Attorneys at Law. Her name should be first. D was better than Lydia for the yellow pages, but then he changed his mind, telling her that it was his name that was so well-known, and she agreed. He wanted a full page ad to run in the newspaper and the yellow pages. Then they went to dinner and drove to the house.

"You're staying now, Danielle."

"Did you work things out for some sort of wedding plan?"

"Of course not. That's a woman's job."

"Then we'll never marry, you lazy ass. Until you can prove to me that you really do want to be my husband, it's not going to happen. But that's fine. You can't get the poor limp thing up anyway."

"What the hell makes you say that?"

"Think about it. How many years has it been? Did you masturbate at all during your imprisonment?"

"Of course not. I mean, I tried. I'd get an erection, but my dick would go limp before I could get it out of my pants. It'd be gone before I could even wrap my hand around it."

"See what I mean, love?"

"We'll see. There just can't be anything better than a Mexican slut to get the old blood boiling." He said, not the least bit concerned about his possible erection problem.

"Is there a lock on my bedroom?"

"Of course not! You don't have a bedroom; we're sharing one big bed and we certainly don't need a lock on any of the doors in the house because you will be where I am, Danielle, and you will always be available to me as a good wife must. Now don't start giving me your old shit about this, like you're some sort of fucking virgin because we both know you ain't no such thing, which is excellent since I find virgins to be a disgusting species; I have to admit that I'm quite happy that some old guy beat me to punch."

They went to an early dinner where they ate, smoked and drank and then they left. Danielle was driving and she went directly to Ace Hardware and bought a door knob with a very sturdy lock, pocketing the key. She'd have to watch her purse carefully. She set to work the minute they got to the house, taking perfect direction on how to replace a door knob from the sales man who was more than happy to help the pretty young lady. He told her that if she had doubts to call a locksmith who would have it in in a New York second. She thanked him and went home, picked one of the rooms to be her new bedroom, and set to work putting in her new doorknob with the very sturdy lock that could only be opened with a key, her key, which she would protect with her life if that's what it took to keep away from that horny idiot.

"Oh shit. You think that little lock is going to keep big ole me out of that room?"

"Yes I do, for two reasons; number one is that I'm not sleeping with you until we're married and number two is that you're too cheap to buy a new door, and you ain't that big anymore either, McNally my man. Just a bag of bones." But he wasn't. She woke to him lying next to her with what she realized was a very healthy erection. He had the lamp on and she lay on top of the covers, naked as a baby.

"Look at that sweet little pussy." He said, rubbing his cheek against it, and sniffing it. "Aw, fresh as a newborn babe. Now this is the life. I always wanted a preteen who just hasn't had the time to mature yet, know what I mean?"

"Why in the hell do men always say that?" She asked, sitting up.

"Men like youth, the younger the better. Hey, where you going?"

"Champagne and cigarettes, Lover Boy."

He joined her and they drank all night long, then she went back to her room, leaving the broken door as it was.

He followed, carrying their bottles of alcohol. She got on the bed, lit a cigarette and took the bottle, drinking from it directly.

When she finished, he took the bottle from her and flipped it over the side onto the floor, his bottle already there.

"Time to enjoy my lovely Latin pussy. I'm not passing this fantasy up for no one."

"You think a good Catholic Mexican would allow a man who wasn't her husband to have sex with her?" She told him that she was going to let her thick Latino pubic hair grow back. That would turn the idiot off and make his little weiner limp again.

"Won't make a difference, my lovely bride." He assured her.

"I'm not your bride, McNally."

As soon as she lay down, he was on top of her, ripping the covers off and jerking the night gown up over her head, letting it float to floor with the bottles. She ignored him. They were both drunk and she was tired as hell. But he ignored her too, pulling her thighs apart. He had waited for years to do this to his timid little receptionist. He got up and went into the bathroom. He found what he wanted and went into the kitchen. When the microwave dinged, he was back, pouring very warm oil all her bare vagina. She ignored him as he licked it off, simply not in the mood for any of this right now.

"You're going to have one hell of a tummy ache, idiot."

"Pure nutrition." He assured her.

She let him lick, enjoying the feeling. Maybe she would keep shaving. She just laid there quite content. Unlike Jan's tongue, his was smooth and very long. He had showed it to her many times, for some reason thinking it would make the little virgin horny or some such ridiculous shit. He tried to move to the sweet spot between her legs, but she crossed them. He waited and when she relaxed, he tried to enter her. She simply kicked him away, and turned her back on him. He stuck his middle finger into her warm moistness and moved it in and out until she slapped his hand away and turned on her stomach.

"I'm Catholic. Go to sleep you drunken idiot."

And he did. She was damned hard work for a drunk.

They spent the weekend lying around the house. McNally followed her around the house from to room as she cleaned and washed all the new sheets and towels that were still in bags and dumped on the living room couch. He followed, drinking coffee and taking dirty, telling what he was going to do her and how he was going to teach her what being a woman really meant. He was going to make her scream and thrash like a happy whore before it was all over, he said. Oh yeah darling, you're gonna really like this. She cleaned and totally ignored him. He kept it up pretty much all morning, following her into the shower and leaning against the wall in his clothes, staying out of the way of the water as he watched her shower. In the afternoon, he took her to lunch and then they went back to the office, he was all business now, thank God.

But he did get her. He was right when he said she had to sleep. What an ass, she thought, remembering her moans and groans and the wild ride, something she hadn't experienced since Jan, but it was even better with Luke, far better, she thought with a smile. He was a wild man and he was so damned much fun. In the office, he was once again business, or so she thought until he threw her on the couch, making her scream and dig her nails into his back once again; just the way she liked it.

A month later, they went downtown to the same old dining room in the same old hotel. He was gaining his weight back and she was glad to see the old Luke slowly emerging but she was tired of the same old places now.

"We really have to find some new places to go. I'm getting sick to death of this one."

"Okay, we'll look. I agree. Maybe we'll find a few good ones that are popping up on the beach. It seems to me like there's a new one every week. It might help to get a little variety back in our boring, sexless life."

He took her to the courthouse and made her fill out the marriage license, warning her not to humiliate him in front of the fine ladies behind the counter.

"Just keep your nasty little mouth shut for once, could ya?

"We don't need to do this, ding dong."

"Shut the fuck up for once." He hissed, not wanting the old ladies to hear her bitching. "I told you, I want a kid."

"I'm sorry to hear that. I can promise you I won't be the mother of any squalling brat of yours. I want my children's daddy to be a real man."

"You have to sleep." Was all he said, his favorite phrase.

Then he tried to drag the sweet Mexican's ass up to the Justice of Peace, but she wasn't having it. There was no flippin way she was getting married in pedal pushers. He took her arm and holding it tight, he dragged her into the department store and forced her to the women's dresses, but she refused to cooperate, just standing there, looking dumb and bored. So he chose a dress and then he went to the shoe department and he bought what he thought was some nice looking heels.

"Those are not appropriate for a wedding."

"Tough shit. You're wearing them tonight while I lick that barefaced pussy of yours.

"So delusional for such a limp dick." She said patting his arm. He paid and they went to the beach to find a new place to eat. Then they sat on the sand and went home. She was absolutely exhausted. She threw the clothes away as soon as she got home. Luke exploded as soon as he saw the trash truck; he instinctively knew what that Mexican whore had done with those very expensive clothes he had bought for her. They had been purchased for her because he wanted to make her happy, determined to give his woman everything she wanted. What a slut!

"You're putting on weight, Danielle. I won't have it!" He said one day at the office, constantly watching her, disgust written all over his ugly stupid face.

"Does that mean I'll finally be free?" She asked sweetly, which he completely ignored.

"I'd let you join me and my gorgeous hookers, but no one wants to see a fat lady naked. I'd be embarrassed."

The tall, slender Italian gangster came in and they got to work, and he remembered all the fun of old; or at least he sure had had a good time. But of course, that was over now, he thought. Maybe with time. He'd wait for a really young buck, or better yet, a gorgeous woman. It surely would be fun to watch the two of them. He knew she'd like it. Maybe he'd surprise her for Christmas. The dumb bitch would never once tell him what she wanted anyway so this would be a gift of his choosing. I can certainly pay for the best, the most experienced, he thought. That was if he even had any money left now that she had been in control of his bank accounts for two years completely unsupervised. Oh yeah, right, he had forgotten what a fucking thief she was. Well, he'd give her the best this time if he could afford it. It'd be a great Christmas all around, especially for little ole me, he thought happily.

He finally forced the stupid woman to the Justice of Peace.

"What the hell? I thought you said pedal pushers weren't appropriate."

"I changed my mind."

"Stupid goddamn Mexican." He hissed just as the old preacher came into the room and was walking toward them, anxious to greet the happy couple on this blessed occasion. He would say the magic words that would seal the lovely young woman's fate, so he hesitated and slowed down now and then in case the woman came to her senses and walked out, but she didn't. No young woman deserved to be talked down to by a man such as this. Life was very strange though, he thought. He had seen it all. So they were married now, the ceremony a fast blur. Danielle went home and McNally went back to the office claiming to have too much work. Oh right, she thought, not the least bit upset about the sad events of this, her wedding day. Thank God. She was just too tired to put up with that idiot tonight.

He poured himself a scotch and then sat down to read the paper, but he couldn't forget the sweet Creole hookers. It had been far too long since he'd been able to enjoy their hot talents. Their bodies put Danielle's to shame, especially now that she was getting fat, plus he had to fight for everything he got from that woman. He called the escort service and two of their most experienced girls came to the office. They drank, they licked, they romped, and he watched cheerfully as he smoked his cigar and drank his fine whiskey. And then it was his turn and the fun began. Eeeee Ha!!

She was tired, and threatened to leave him there whenever she came to transcribe a tape.

"Goddamn it! Get that fucking tape typed." He demanded, yelling at her from his lovely desk. He had missed it far more than he missed that whore in the outer office. Some things just plain didn't change at all, he thought, so frustrated once again with the stupid bitch. She always had to argue about every little thing, for God's sake!

She would simply get up and walk out to the car and drive off, but he didn't follow. It was cold and he was happy. He had whiskey and wine for the girls and plenty of beer. The week was set. And he clicked on his phone. He knew the number by heart.

She met her gynecologist at the hospital on Christmas Eve to settle in before labor started, if it even would, you just never knew with first time pregnancies Dr. Gloria had told her. She had kept all her appointments and accepted a shot so that milk wouldn't form, not sure she wanted to be tied down with a baby at her breast right now, especially when she had so much typing to do, and they were working to get the business back up and running. She had chosen her doctor randomly from the yellow pages when she finally figured out that she was pregnant and because she accepted her insurance and could see her fairly soon, she decided that this woman would be her doctor through her pregnancy. They became instant friends, comrades in the never ending challenges of womanhood. They went to the cafeteria today and ate and then drank reams of coffee.

"Let's go smoke." Gloria said, knowing that her patient turned pal was a smoker.

"You're nuts. It's freezing out there."

"No, no, trust me sister, I have a very nice, very warm hiding place."

"Does this place have wine?"

"Not yet, but it will by this evening. I just have to run to the store."

"Well, don't waste your time smoking, friend. Without wine, it's just not that much fun, if you ask me."

They went to her office and lit up, happy and comfortable as they talked about the birth.

"The baby is large, but don't worry. I'm on it." She said, puffing away to the ceiling. "But it's gonna hurt like hell coming out, of course."

"Oh shit. Just like its father. I sure hope it doesn't act like him."

"If it's a boy, there's a very good chance that he will. Well, I'm out of here. I've got one more young lady to see before I can call it a day and close up the office." The doctor said as she put out her cigarette and stood up.

Danielle turned on TV and read on her hospital bed. Gloria came back and had the box of white wine because her pregnant friend asked for it, her favorite. She stuck the box and plastic wine glasses in the cabinet and left. Danielle read. She knew McNally was with his hookers. He had been talking about it for days going into great detail about how they wanted to please their man, unlike his bride of course. Good for him, she thought, glad for the reprieve from the half-wit.

Gloria came back and they drank and smoked while they waited. She brought a small air cleaner from her office and it hummed happily, just thrilled for something to do.

Gloria left and she went into labor. No one came to give her a shot. It wasn't on the chart, the cold-hearted nurse told her. She screamed for at least four hours; but Gloria was asleep, too busy, too much wine, just worn out. She woke in a panic and ran to Danielle, but she had a boy on her chest, blood spurting from between her legs everywhere. She instructed the orderly to ready her for surgery and she ran to ready an operating room. Danielle went to intensive care when she left surgery, her poor vagina now full of stitches from the huge tear the boy had opened when he entered the world through her small body. Unfortunately, she was still unconscious from the anesthesia. Gloria hadn't been able wake her up, but she was confident that she'd come around by morning. They always did. But she didn't. She called her husband and gave him the attorney's office address and asked him to drive out there and tell him about his son.

Dr. Paul, Gloria's husband, and McNally came to the hospital mid-morning and the nurse brought his boy into the room and he fed his son. The dumb bitch didn't think he knew, but he knew way before she did. Paul had come to the office and told him that he had a son, and the good doctor got rather tipsy as the night wore on, becoming instant friends with McNally, just like Gloria and Danielle.

"What a life." McNally said, feeding his little boy. "You just can't trust a broad, Paul."

Gloria ignored them, wondering if it had been a good idea to introduce these two, but they were so different from one another, she was sure that their budding relationship, or whatever it was, would sizzle and then go out as quickly as it had started. She was certainly not going to discourage it; however, they looked like they were fast becoming good buddies, all for the love of stupid football of course, and her husband had so few friends she was glad that he had found someone he could perhaps spend some time with to at least watch football, obviously a love they shared man to man and she certainly had no intention of discouraging him from spending time with his new football buddy.

Danielle wasn't waking. She was in a coma, she told McNally. He handed the baby to the nurse, his face white and his hands shaking. He was alone in the room where his wife should be lying, holding her son.

"No God. No please. I'll never look at another woman. I promise God. Please just don't take my Danielle. He went into the intensive care unit and took her hand, overwhelmed by a quiet desperation and pleading for her life. She found him. They needed each other. Please God!!

He stayed there most of the night until Paul came and convinced him to come back in the morning. He didn't want to go home, but Paul and Gloria each took an arm and led the sad, heartbroken man out to the car. He'd stay with them until Danielle either died or came home. Gloria was stunned at this man's obvious sadness; she had no idea that this man actually loved her friend. From what Danielle had told her, she was surprised at his reaction to the possibility that his wife might not make it through this. She had thought that he was nothing more than a cold hearted attorney who cared for no one but himself and the endless hookers Danielle had told her about. How wrong could she possibly be, she asked herself as she walked with him to their car. This was such a sad, sad night for everyone. She was losing someone she would miss terribly even though they hadn't known each other for very long, she thought, feeling such a deep sense of regret that she couldn't have done something more to save her young friend's life.

She was with her grandmother, just like the stories she had heard. She climbed a dark staircase, and there she was. Her mother, her grandmother and so many others mixed amongst the angels and the stars and the flowers. She and her grandmother and her mother roamed freely, running and lifting up into the clouds. They danced and laughed. No one ate. No one needed food. Only wine, which flowed freely, carried by the angels. But there would be a banquet soon, her grandmother assured her. It was wonderful and everyone was there. The table flowed across the stars forever. Everyone was happy. The angels hovered and sang so sweetly. Then her grandmother and sweet mother walked on the deep emerald grass and they sat down together by the beautiful blue river as the breeze blew gently and the butterflies drifted from one beautiful flower to another. I love you Papa, she said to her grandfather. I've missed you so very much. But he just smiled and disappeared into the throng of long ago ancestors who had made it through the beautiful pearly gates. So many!

"You must go now, Danielle."

"No, Grandma." Her mother looked down at her daughter's sweet, sweet face.

"Yes, you must go back; you have a son now. You must go now. If you don't, your husband will die tragically. He can't live without you Danielle.

Danielle got up and rushed to her grandmother and then her mother kissing them good-bye. Then she ran as fast as she could. The angels grabbed her and lifted her into the dark sky, amongst the stars that twinkled brightly.

Danielle woke in her bed. She sat up and looked at the needle in her arm. She pulled it out gently and went to the cafeteria; she had never been so hungry in her life. She got a tray and piled it with food that she charged to her room and moved to the very back of the cafeteria to a small table. She wished she had her book, but she didn't. She ate and finished it off with wonderful apple dumplings floating in a beautiful buttery warm cinnamon sauce and she drank cup after cup of coffee.

She took her tray back and ordered a to-go cup of coffee. She sipped it as she walked very slowly back to her room. She had to see her baby, a son her mother had said.

The intensive care nurse was almost hysterical. She rushed to the front desk and called Gloria. "Danielle McNally is gone, Gloria."

"Gone?"

"Yes, she's gone! Someone took the needle out of her arm and carried her somewhere."

"Okay. Just calm down. Her husband probably took her home. Let me call home. He was supposed to spend the day with my husband."

She talked to Paul. Nope, McNally was right here.

"Get him down here now. Danielle is missing and no one can find her."

Why on earth she wanted McNally here was beyond her, and then Gloria went back to her office and waited. The woman couldn't just disappear. She called the nursery. No, she hadn't been there to see the baby, the nurse said. She hung up. There was nothing else to do. She'd wait for the men and then call the police. They were there in 20 minutes.

"Paul you get back to the boys." She said putting her arms around her husband.

"We'll find her, Gloria. Just relax and don't worry."

"I'll go to the nursery and then to her room. I'll be there until we find her. If you need me, you'll know where to find me." McNally said, all business now.

The police came, took a report and left, looking around the parking lot first. Nothing. She'd turn up. Gloria went to the physician's sleeping room and went to sleep. She was absolutely exhausted now. She had been up most of the night working the ER night shift. She was getting too old for this damned schedule!

McNally went to his son and held him, sitting in the rocking chair in the nursery. He'd take him home tomorrow. He'd be a good father if Herrera disappeared and could never be found. He wondered about Jan. He knew where to go. He'd find her just like she found him, and with that thought he relaxed. Everything was going to be okay.

When the baby finished eating and was burped, he laid him in the incubator and went to Danielle's room to wait. She was reading, looking healthy as any angel. When she saw him, she sat up and waited for him to sit and then she jumped down and threw herself into his lap and began kissing her man. They held onto each other, never wanting to let go. She was here now and he vowed to protect this woman with his life as he held onto her, a drowning man holding onto the life jacket that would keep his head above water.

"My beautiful Danielle. Please don't ever leave me again. I just couldn't take it. I couldn't." He said quietly.

Danielle felt the tears slide down her cheeks as he held her so tight. "My God, McNally, my God. You keep leaving me. I love you so much."

"Does this mean you'll finally fuck me, my lovely bride with that bare assed little girl's pussy?" He asked seriously.

"Shut the hell up, McNally!" She said, pushing him away and snapping out of her disgusting display of love for this stupid, stupid half-wit. "You'd ruin a wet dream. Now go get the baby and let's get the hell out of here, you Prick. I never should have married you."

She huffed, walking to the closet where her clothes were. She was so disgusted! She should never have married that nut case. She'd file for divorce as soon as she got home, she vowed.

He watched her from the chair. "Well, here the bitch is. Right on schedule." He said to her.

"Yeah, well fuck you and your horse and your hookers."

He laughed and went to get his son. It served the woman right. If she couldn't take care of her man, well then she'd just have to pay the consequences, he thought happily. He grabbed a wheelchair and wheeled it into the room and put the very not so tiny newborn in her arms. Then he called a cab and wheeled her out of there. The nursery nurse hadn't even seen him take the baby. Too bad, so sad.

The cab came quickly and he took them home. He called Paul, who answered on the first ring and told him he had his wife and son, but Gloria wasn't answering her phone. She was very likely sound asleep or maybe in surgery her husband told him.

And they went home to champagne, cigarettes and whiskey. And of course the cold rain and the flash of lightning that lit up the sky and ended with the loud crack of thunder that resounded throughout the day. This was her earth's heaven now and she wanted the storm to last forever.

Gloria called the next morning and she and Danielle talked.

"Geez, bitch. Get off the phone," he yelled. You'll see her tomorrow."

"Shut the fuck up, Prick." She shouted.

"Well, I see the happy family is now intact."

"Oh my God, Gloria, why didn't I die? Let's go shopping tomorrow."

"You're on!"

"More money?" McNally said, walking to the coffee pot. "Does it ever end with you?"

When the coffee finished, she picked up the cup and dumped it in the sink as her beautiful man watched, slamming the heavy coffee cup on the counter. "Nope." She said.

He disgustedly pulled another pod. These little babies were just too damned expensive to be wasting like that, he fumed.

And she went to her son and fed him, amazed at how much he looked like his daddy, not a speck of Mexican as far as she could tell. They lay around all day not wanting to go out into the cold morning air and subject their son to that just yet. She wore her ridiculous granny nightgown and the slippers with the puppy dog ears flopping and the tail out the back of the slippers which she constantly stepped on. He wanted her to fall to the ground, he thought. He needed a good laugh right about now.

Eventually, she got a pillow and blanket and lay down on the couch, putting her bare feet in his lap. He idly rubbed them as he watched the game. Right on cue, she thought. It had been such a long, long time since anyone had rubbed her feet.

He went to the office, claiming he had clients. Yeah, right. Talk about expensive, she told him.

He called at 4 that afternoon. "There are three tapes here on my desk." he informed her.

"And one in the recorder, right?"

"Okay, four tapes."

"Are you coming home tonight, or do hookers call?"

"I'm leaving now. Then we're going to fuck. I'm sick of your innuendos, you little Mexican whore. Time to take care of your man."

He was home in 20 minutes, even though he drove slowly in the pounding rain. Like Danielle, he loved this weather, remembering his years of imprisonment.

He took a shower and shaved. Danielle was dressed warmly in a big cream colored sweater and her wool maternity wool leggings. They didn't fit her any more, stretched to their limit by her beach ball belly, but she found an old an old belt made of cloth that she could tie around her still tender stomach. She put on her small diamond necklace, not having a clue why she ever took it off, and then grabbed her watch. She put on her makeup as her husband watched her spray her face with some sort of mist, wondering how much that cost him. But the wench was a number 10, he thought.

She wrapped the baby and belted him into the infant seat, and threw McNally his coat.

"Wear it. You're a father now and you have responsibilities. Pneumonia ain't one of them."

They didn't want to go too far from home with their newborn, and so they ended up in a very brightly lit restaurant where parents and children sat at most tables, obviously a restaurant that catered to families and noisy children.

"See they have babies." He said. What an idiot. Who cared if there were babies, she asked him, quite snotty, actually.

They ordered, she an absolutely delicious burrito and very small salad and he his porter, of course. As they ate she told him of her death. He listened, not saying anything as he cut and ate. He remembered the hell, the sobbing and the promises. His God had answered them and he was so thankful, falling on his knees every night in the privacy of the nursery. He promised that his little family would start church at the chapel down the road. Well, maybe not right away though.

"My grandmother and grandfather and mother were there. For some reason, I didn't talk to my Papa though. We walked and we laughed and flew to the clouds with the angel that carried such beautiful wines for us."

She told him of the angels and the singing and floating amongst the stars and the grass and the flowers and the sparkling blue river and butterflies.

"My mother told me it was time to go home now because I had a son and that McNally loved me. If I didn't leave, my McNally would not live long. I ran; let me tell you, I ran until I was back in my bed."

"Yeah, well, the old broad is just a bunch of useless bones buried 6 feet under. Obviously you were delusional."

"No, Luke, you're wrong."

"Where'd you go?"

"Down to the cafeteria. I was starving." She said, as she finished her burrito and started on her wine.

"You going to the office tomorrow?"

"Yep. I'll be in court the whole day."

"Will you come home?"

"Of course I'll come home. Who else is going to feed and change my son?"

"Well, I can do it if you're going to be busy with your expensive hookers. You always said they made me look fat."

"Yeah, not anymore though. You'll do just fine. Just don't shave your twat."

"How romantic, McNally. I see your love for me has made you more sensitive."

"Yep." He said shoving in a really too big piece of meat."

"You're a pig."

"Yep."

Then they went home to wine, Chivas Regal and cigarettes and this time he had Cuba's finest cigars, illegal of course. She read; he watched football. He didn't touch the wench. Gloria had threatened him rather harshly to his way of thinking. He was not to touch her best friend if he wanted to live to see another day. Best friends now, huh? Go figure. You never could figure out a woman. They were all fucking crazy. Ask any man.

"Geez Lady. I just don't need this right now. I want my wife and I want her now."

"That's just too bad. I mean it Luke. You will lose your football buddy if you dare to make a move on her until she's healed. Six weeks Pal, not one day sooner."

"My God. Women just aren't worth it, Paul."

"Just keep your dick in your pants and make sure your bride is on birth control. Ya all will be just fine and dandy."

"Good advice, that."

"Talk to Gloria. She's the lady with the pills."

"Can't you write a prescription for her, Paul?"

"I suppose that I could, but she isn't my patient. I work mostly with men who have reproductive system problems. Urologists don't usually write for birth control and she would have to come to my office to be examined; however, I'm not equipped with the proper instruments for a pelvic examination. So, you're stuck with Gloria Bud."

So he had to wait. It was going to be a long winter, he thought, totally ignoring her as she read. Let's see, it's been just at 3 weeks now, he thought, but the baby kept them busy and the time flew.

Business was booming and they would go to the office and meet with the clients. Danielle would type and he would change diapers and order lunch. Then they'd go home to another cozy night with the fire dancing in the fireplace and football dancing on the large TV in the living room.

On the first day marking the end of the 6 weeks, he celebrated, following her around, talking dirty. When she picked up her book, he'd take it from her.

"You need to listen to your man, wench." He'd say. "This is your duty and I'm here to collect."

When she'd go to the shower he'd follow, kicking off his precious boots first, whiskey in his hand and a cigar in his mouth. She always took a shower when he was in this mood because she loved for him to stand in the corner and talk dirty. Who did that? Her man did, obviously. He was definitely one in a million. God, she loved that stupid shit. She had stopped bleeding weeks ago, but she didn't mention it, telling Gloria to keep her mouth shut.

"Good luck." Gloria said with a smirk.

He followed her out and sat on the bed in his wet jeans until she jerked him up off the bed, her titties bouncing. He tried his best to suck a nipple, but she grabbed the sheets and the bedspread and took them to the washer.

"Take care of your son. He's crying to be fed. And change his diapers this time. And name the boy, goddamnit, he's not a fucking orphan!"

And he would. He would feed him and then rock him back to sleep. Then he'd follow her and start again. She'd lay on the couch with her book and he'd get up and toss it behind the couch or across the room. She'd sigh and close her eyes as he spread her legs, but then she'd turn and knock him off the small space his ass covered as he perched precariously on the edge of the couch next to her. He'd go back to his whiskey and cigar.

"You have to sleep sometime, Princess." He predicted once again.

"Yes, I do with a knife under the pillow."

"Okay, thanks for letting me know, Bitch."

She woke to a wet tongue and moaning, hers. He rode her once again and she moaned and dug her nails in happily. It had been so long, far too long.

He rode her nightly, making up for time lost, usually while she slept of course, jerking her from her deep sleep, which really, really pissed her off! But sometimes she'd kneel down as he watched his endless ball games and pull his limp penis from his zipper. He would be surprised of course, but within seconds, his flabby member would stand to attention and sing with joy. And then the rain came down and the flowers bloomed.

She was pregnant. He saw the pouch and watched it for a while. Goddamn it, here we go again. Six weeks of hell. He called Gloria and told her to examine the dumb bitch.

"I'm not gonna have a useless cunt lying around the house because she complains nonstop to be exhausted. It would drive any man to murder the stupid lazy-assed bitch." He informed his wife's doctor.

"Oh my goodness. What a man. I so wish my Paul was more like you."

Then he talked to Paul about the latest game. They had no idea ever which team was playing which team. Who gave a shit? There were long-legged black boys and they had a ball and those son-a-bitches could run!

They met at her office and she asked her sex dates.

"Beats the hell out of me. I sure didn't have time to look at a calendar, believe me. Just show me the bed, please."

"Okay, it was Christmas and the end of the 6th week will take us into middle February." She said looking at her desk calendar.

"Aw shit! I'm honestly going to have to kill him. The bastard just won't leave me alone. I don't know how much more of his shit I can take."

"Here's liquid iron. Take it twice a day. Here's your prenatals. Now wake up, we've got to go shopping."

She didn't say anything to McNally. But he never touched her. He wanted to live. The baby was due very likely sometime in late January or early February. And of course she slept and ate everything in sight. But the bitch could still type, and that was all he needed from his bride. She got so fat, she waddled. He couldn't believe it. Would she ever be normal again he asked her daily, watching her in horror as she grew and just wanting her to go far, far away where he didn't have to look at her anymore.

"Fuck you, McNally and your fucking horse too." She said, feeling his eyes on her.

She lived in the bathroom this time. This baby was hell on her very small bladder. She worked, she painted, she bought more baby furniture for the empty nursery she had chosen for this baby; she waddled, she peed, she smoked just a little, and had an occasional glass of wine throughout the spring, summer and autumn. The pumpkins were carved and on every door step and then it was Christmas, but she was too big and too tired to care. But it sped by far too quickly and she went into labor. This time he took her to the hospital and sat right there. He informed Gloria that he wasn't going to leave for any amount of money. She was absolutely not going to disappear this time. It truly surprised her. The fool really did love her after all, she thought with a grin as she walked out of the room. The man never ceased to surprise her.

She screamed and cussed as he and Paul watched, just fascinated. He held her hand like any good husband would, trying to bring comfort to his woman and looked into her open mouth as she screamed bloody murder. She bit his hand and he pulled it fast.

"What a bitch, man." He said to Paul who really enjoyed that. His wife had always suffered quietly as he read or watched football beside her.

"Fun huh?"

"Sure is."

"Get out of here, both of you!" Gloria demanded, coming in to check on her friend's progress once again, but they ignored her, entranced by the woman writhing on the bed. She shook her head and walked out of the room. This wasn't going to end anytime soon for her poor, poor friend. Maybe she'd agree to get on birth control this time.

She took forever, but finally she popped out the infant. This was definitely a Mexican he thought as the nurse laid the tiny baby on his wife's gorgeous titties. He didn't mind that Paul looked. Eat your heart out friend he told him. Yeah, they're nice alright.

"Oh my God! Will you two shut the hell up for once!" Danielle yelled at them and the nurse laughed. This had been the most fun she'd ever had in the labor room.

She took the baby, and Danielle covered herself immediately and fell sound asleep, holding McNally's hand. And then three hours later, he heard loud moaning, her face bright red as she pushed and then cried out. He pulled the sheet back and there she was with another little cutie pie, a little fatty, just like his other boy.

"Oh my God! I just can't do this now!" She shouted at the ceiling. But he was here and he wasn't going to leave her, he said, picking up the newest little boy who had popped out, demanding to be fed at the top of his lungs. He picked him up and rang for the nurse and she once again was taken to surgery to be stitched up like new again.

"I'm outta here." Gloria said. "Just leave the babies with the nurses. You'll very likely take them home sometime tomorrow. As soon as you can walk again, you and I are going to lunch, she said to her friend.

Gloria kissed Danielle's forehead and congratulated her on the birth of her boys, and then she left with her husband.

The nurse brought in a very comfortable recliner for McNally and a blanket and he watched football. They took the babies home the next morning. He wouldn't let Danielle or the nanny she had hired touch them.

"No, no woman. Scoot on out. I got this." She'd shake her head and say Lord have mercy and go to Danielle.

"That man is sure gonna be a father to be proud of; I tell ya, I've never seen anything like this before. Bless his nasty little heart." Danielle would smile. It was true.

Then the dirty talk started, the moans and screams, the wild bronco riding.

"When you gonna learn McNally?"

"You're on birth control. Ain't a thing to worry about." He said, the cigar clamped in his teeth, Chivas Regal and football waited.

Stupid, stupid idiots; all the male species who roamed the earth, dragging their dicks from one woman to the next, she thought with disgust.

"Want to make a bet?" She said, moving past the couch to the kitchen. He picked up the phone and called Gloria.

"My wife informs me that she is not on the pill. Did you tie her tubes like I asked?

"I can't do that without Danielle's permission, my man."

"But you'll give her the pills tomorrow, right?"

"Yep. I've got them in my purse as we speak." She lied.

They went shopping, they talked, they shopped, they went swimming and target practice in the building next the gun shop. They went scuba diving in the bay.

She was pregnant, she told him happily, twirling, obviously drunk. She had a bottle of champagne clutched in her skinny hands and had been drinking it for heaven knew how long. She plopped in his lap and tipped the bottle to her mouth, foam spurting from her nose.

He pushed her off. "You're making me sick! Stupid drunk!" He said, watching her foaming nose with disgust as it dripped the damned expensive champagne, what a waste!! He sat her down hard beside him.

"Best Christmas present ever, I mean for you! Not me! I'll be free to play, play, play." She sang as she jumped up and twirled in front of the TV.

"Move out of the way you stupid Mexican!" A game was on Goddamnit!

"I can't do this anymore you stupid drunken slut! I clean and change diapers and I have to feed the stinking screaming brats on top of all that. And look at you, drinking like this with an innocent baby in your belly. It's going to be born a half-wit thanks to you! You're a no good drunk, Danielle!" He fumed, totally ignoring the fact that they had a very capable nanny who would be more than happy to take care of the brats. "I'll leave your ass and I won't be back." He warned her, his hands on her small drunk shoulders, shaking her. He thought about popping her in the jaw, but...well... "I'm going to beat you and then I'm leaving first thing in the morning."

"Let me pack for you, you fucking loser." She slurred angrily, staggering to the bedroom. He heard the closet open and the suitcase zipper scream loudly. He would let her pack all his clothes. It would save him time.

"I'm so happy." She sang when she was finished throwing his crap into the big suitcase. She had come back to the living room just to torment him, he thought, trying his best to ignore the stupid drunk. She was twirling, her arms in the air, holding the bottle. She drank and plopped down on the couch next to him.

"You can fuck your beautiful Creole escorts and I can have fun with the clients. Remember? What fun. And the best part is that I won't have to dole out 100s of dollars. They would gladly pay me, can you believe that McNally?"

"Why in God's name did I ever marry a Mexican?" He lamented to the ceiling, looking for God somewhere. Everyone knew they were cruel, not even blinking an eye when they shoved that sharp blade into their men, twisting for good measure. He had asked God this many times. But then he turned to the television as the crowds roared. Good game, man!

She woke sick as a dog the next morning. He absolutely refused to go to the drug store to get the precious Advil for her no matter how much she begged, truly unable to drive anywhere herself with this nausea and unrelenting pounding headache. She called Charlene into her bedroom and sent her off to the drugstore, thanking God that the woman was there to help her. She also promised God that she would not touch another drop until this baby was born. What McNally said had hit home more than he knew.

Stupid drunk he muttered as he walked out the door and went to breakfast. Ah shit, he forgot the suitcase. Then he went to work. Just more murdering scum-bag clients claiming innocence. Stupid fucking Wops. He had had it with everything and everyone. Wops, Irish

gang members and especially Mexicans. He was going
to buy a boat and sail far away.

And she grew and she waddled and she pissed
nonstop. She kept busy with the next room, this time
painting it pink and buying a little girl crib and all
the pink pajamas and tiny dresses she loved for her
daughter, or maybe daughters, the way things were
going lately. Then once again she screamed for hours.
This time, she popped out two, her little girl, finally!
And they took them straight to nursery, thank God.
Time to go shopping she told Gloria completely drained.
Thank God she didn't have to breast feed. With every
pregnancy, Gloria would give her a shot before the milk
glands could form, so she was free from that at least.
There was no way she could breast feed and type the
notes McNally needed. She was stitched up once again,
slept for two days and then went home.

The third nursery was ready and she carried her
burdens into the house. He didn't help of course. He
ignored the newborn babies, not wanting to even look
at them, not at all interested. Too many for one man to
have carry through life. He'd be old and worn out way
before his time and he'd have to work his fingers to the
bone just to feed so many of them. He was done, he said,
as she went into nursery and plopped them down.

"You'll have to feed them. They're all yours now
McNally. Maybe you'll finally learn to save your dick for
your lovely bouncing hookers."

It was a warn spring day and the pool was so lovely. She and Gloria and the nanny lay around, swimming and then lying in the beautiful warm afternoon sun, talking idly. The men sat in comfortable lounge chairs at the table. Whiskey and cigars. Always stupid smelly cigars, phalluses probably, she told Gloria. "You just may be on to something here." Gloria agreed.

The sun was so warm on her pale white skin.

"Gloria, why on earth do I keep having multiple births? I just don't understand any of this."

"It would certainly be familial. Multiple births usually run in the family line. Are there multiple births in your family?"

"God, who knows?"

"Get on birth control, Danielle. That will certainly put a stop to having to go through this again....you know, the miracles of modern medicine, Girl." She told her, not really understanding why she never did.

Paul compared the two women idly, so different! One had a lovely curly soft cap and one had lank, thinning hair becoming more and more obvious with time. He wondered why and so did Gloria of course. She didn't have enough hair anymore to cover her scalp. It was mousy brown and so thin now and streaked with grey at the temples. He wondered why because she was young still. It was probably just the stress of being a doctor perhaps. She was certainly busier than he had ever been. She was definitely starting to bald on top, but she sure had long, long slender legs, all legs, but no boobs. They had disappeared long ago with the three very hungry boys; working breasts she would tell him. But she was okay. Who needed boobs when there were lovely legs to wrap around your waist? Not him! Danielle's lovely, rather large breasts sure didn't do her any good. Her husband didn't even like her. What the hell was wrong with the man, he often wondered. He was just born a jerk, some weird accident of birth very likely. But the man sure did like those beautiful escorts, as he so often told him and with time, he finally agreed to join him at his office. Two to a man, Dude. He thought about it often and he knew he would. It would certainly be fun. Yep, just a jerk from birth and he planned to tag right along with him.

And he eventually did join in on the fun. All they had to do was lay back and watch the women, two to one, sucking licking until he thought his penis would explode. He went often, usually every Saturday while the women shopped, sometimes staying most of the night with the women, telling Gloria he was on call at the hospital. Always different, sometimes black as midnight or the color of coffee with cream, sometimes blond and blue eyed. So many, so young and firm. Bouncing around, licking each other as they watched. Young muscular men with huge penises came too. At first he resisted, just watching, but certainly wanting to, his knees weak with a desire that couldn't be quenched any other way, but not anymore, oh no! Not now. Tight as virgins, their sweet hairy rectums were. Was he queer he asked himself? Yep. He could never get enough of them. Young and strong as they pounded into him. So nice! He began to look at men in the street, driving to the hookers if the male escorts weren't available, but this was before he was introduced to the gay men's club and wash houses. Yep, definitely more fun, no silly game playing here. They got right down to business and never had to see each other, just a hole in the wall that he would back up to. He just couldn't get enough. Gloria very likely knew, but she could care less. Maybe she even had her own little friends. She sure as hell never showed any sexual interest in him, always available to him of course, but he sensed a great reluctance on her part, thinking about the work that needed to be completed or dinner that had to be prepared, so he had pretty much stopped approaching her, but it never even crossed his mind to have an affair with a willing nurse or anything like that, until now of course. He was a very happy man. He had never been one to moan or show any emotion during their sex, but oh my Lord had all of that changed.

And she did suspect what Paul was doing. Who cared? Her husband was happy as a lark. Leave him alone. He never talked to her about it or tried to give her the details of his partying, so really, who cared? And if her teenaged boys found out, well, they'd just have to learn to accept their father on his terms. Nothing wrong with a little variety in an otherwise rather boring life.

The men gazed at their brides, lying so brightly in the lovely, sunny afternoon. No Goddamn football anywhere. Son-of-a-bitch! What the hell? Nothin nowhere, not even on cable. And they sure as hell weren't going to watch baseball. Just no good. So they watched their wives lying in the sun.

"I'm so jealous of you, Danielle." She said; the sun so warm, making them so lazy, almost falling asleep.

"Me? Why? You want my big handsome husband now, is that it?" And they grinned into the beautiful warm spring sun.

"Your big bosom, your hair, your lush lips, your soft skin."

"Good lord, Gloria. There are plastic surgeons and skin spas everywhere. Pick one and we'll go together. I've never gotten to go to a spa and be pampered. We'll go."

"I guess. I've thought about it, believe me. Pride keeps me from going to have any surgery done I think. I just don't want the whole medical community to know and to gossip and speculate my motives. You wouldn't believe the gossip at the hospital. Everyone thrives on it, especially the nurses. Someone would spread the word within minutes."

"So, let's got to New York City."

"Yes!" She said, perking up.

"Come on, let's go look and make the appointment. What exactly would you have done?"

"Everything. Hair implants. Light blond hair with lighter streaks, lips, nose, and maybe those clear braces that no one can see; my teeth are crooked and I certainly don't have a nice smile, and all that damned coffee and tea I'm constantly drinking doesn't help because they seem to be permanently yellowed no matter how often I brush with whitening toothpaste. It's just amazing that I actually found a husband, but of course I was younger and had more hair and actually had a little bit of a breast. But now they're just old useless teats that just sort of hang there on my chest for no good reason at all. I'm thinking I'd like to have them enlarged to at least as big as yours. With my height, I should be able to handle a pretty good size; not too big though, I don't want to look like a hooker, just a nice size and firm, and then of course suction for the cellulite. I'd like to find a way to get rid of the loose skin on my thighs, but the scars are horrible from that sort of surgery."

"There's a new procedure that I was reading about where they heat the skin and then freeze it. It's completely nonsurgical and only takes an hour or two. WA-LA, tight as a teenager again; so you can definitely have that done to your face and neck and stomach and thighs, just about everywhere you think you might want it; it's supposed to tighten everything right up. On the down side, you have to have it done every two or three years, but really, it would be so worth it, especially because there is absolutely no down time. I'm sure that you won't have to run to New York for that, especially if we join a gym and work out faithfully. If we do that, you may not have to have it done again anyway, but if you still want to, if someone finds out, who cares? You'll be young and you'll be lovely and that's what counts. You certainly can't live your life according to what other people think of you.

"Okay, that's a really wonderful idea. I'll do some research and make a decision then, especially for my stomach and my skinny, creppy-skinned thighs. My legs from the knees down are fine, I think."

"Oh my God, this is going to be so much fun! Come on. New York City here we come!"

She told Charlene their plans, but McNally had gone back to his office so he wasn't around when she was getting ready to leave for New York City; however, Charlene agreed that she would let him know her plans as soon as he came back home.

There was one appointment after another. First the hair implants which would take a little time to grow of course and once they were at a decent growth, she'd go to the beautician. This would take a little time, but she was more than happy to wait for her hair to grown in.

"We'll keep the bandages on your scalp for a few days and give you a course of antibiotics." The doctor said. Her hairline and the top of her head were filled with little shoots of the hair that had been taken from different sections of her scalp. She was quite surprised that they were able to gather so many from her thin scalp. "Just give it a month or so to really see the difference. Eventually new hair will blend with the rest of the hair and it will be wonderfully thick, which will be permanent of course. Just be patient. You can go back to work in a week and no one will be the wiser. If there is a problem or you want even thicker hair, just give us a call."

And then off to the dentist where the clear inserts were placed. She had trouble talking, spitting more than she liked every time she spoke! No, you'll get used to them. Just take them out when you eat if it's something like steak or salad. I'll live on baked potatoes and apple sauce, she told Danielle.

"Me too. I love those and lots of bread."

That's not conducive to health, Danielle. We need lots of raw fruit and vegetables."

"Okay, we can do that easily but don't ever suggest that I give up prime rib and creamy horseradish, and oh yes, yes the warm bread with lots of creamy butter. Baby back ribs, here we come! If we join a gym and we walk, it won't be a problem anyway."

They spent close to a month in New York City. First it was the anesthesia for the breast implants and then anesthesia again for the nose and lips procedures; which took a while for her to regain her strength back from the anesthesia, and of course she was in some pain. All these ugly bandages across my nose, Danielle! Who knew? When will my black eyes go away? Soon. Look they're lightening now as we speak. Lips, so lovely. Just like Danielle's now. She had a nice little brown mole right there beside her lip that was all hers.

"When will I start to look lovely? Do you have any idea how long it will take?" She asked her friend impatiently.

"I have an idea. Let's go to one of the islands in the Caribbean while I heal. Of course you've been gone for a while. I'm sure you want to get back to the babies. I know I sure would."

"But I'm not worried about them. They have their nanny and she takes care of everything so there really isn't much I have to do with the kids, and McNally still hasn't come home, but Birdie is there with them. I know they're well taken care of so as long as they're cuddled when they're fed and their diapers are changed, I don't think my presence one way or another will make one damn bit of difference to them at this point, except for Morgan of course, but he's almost three years old now and he thinks Charlene is his mommy anyway; he always has. The other two are 18 months now and then of course the two youngest are still so little. I haven't been much of a hands on mommy, but once we're done here, I don't plan to ever leave any of my babies to other people again, so let's have fun now and then I will get down to the business of raising my children, with or without that bastard McNally." It was time to scuba dive again. She called Charlene and warned her that she'd be gone for a few more weeks. The babies were fine, she said, and growing like weeds.

"Is Luke there yet?"

"No. He was gone when you left and he's never been back. I don't think he even knows that you're gone because he hasn't call here once. Pretty busy in court I guess."

But she didn't want to think about that now. The man obviously had no intention of settling down or being a family man, but she'd cross that bridge later.

"I'm sure you need a break Charlene. I know I would by now. Is there someone you can call to help you? Someone you trust so that you can get out of the house for a while?"

Yes, she said she already called her girlfriend's daughter. She was really a great help and she loved being with the babies when she came to see them. She was always there, holding them and helping her feed them.

"Okay. Let me know how much you want to pay her if she agrees to help. I'll be home in about two weeks."

So off they went. They dove in skimpy suits, the young crew of healthy men watching, waiting, eyes shiny as they stared, their tongues hanging out as the girls lie half naked on the lounge chairs, basking in the lovely sun under a sapphire sea. They ignored them; grabbing a towel and covering themselves when they saw how it was affecting them. Sex was just not for them they agreed, but it was cruel and nasty of them to entice those young men for no reason at all. They just hadn't given it much of a thought actually. Who on earth cared anyway? Obviously these hungry young men, Gloria said lazily. We need to stay fully dressed from now on and they did.

She told her about Jan, about her years without McNally, about how she found him.

"My goodness, Danielle! You've never mentioned any of this!"

"Yeah, it was a long time ago. That's when I got pregnant with my first boy."

"God, I can just imagine! You were probably starving for him."

"Yes, yes I was. He would harass me nonstop at work, trying to get me to have sex, clients, escorts, you name it. And here I was, a sweet 15 year old virgin, but he sure as hell didn't know that. He'd whine and tell me that all he wanted was to make me lie on the couch so he could watch me with this person or that. He was truly a half-wit and out of his mind. So then, of course, he'd fire me and tell me I was just no good for his office and he wanted someone with a little more experience. I'd just ignore him and write a big check for my growing savings account." They laughed happily as she told the story to her friend. Such fond memories Gloria, she said.

"You know, the stupid ass follows me into the shower, fully clothed, whiskey bottle in his hand and a cigar in his teeth."

"What? Why the hell would anyone do that?"

"I'm telling you, Gloria darling, he's not just a sex maniac, the guys got a screw lose."

"Yes, so you've said many times. But you adore him. He loves you like no one ever could. It's just him being charming, as odd as that may seem to us normal folk, Danielle."

"Mankind is doomed then. All he does is bitch about what a lazy Mexican slut I am and how much work he has to do with his useless kids, all nasty Mexicans, just useless. And of course he had his hookers. He has no intention of giving those up."

They laughed together on that beautiful afternoon, drinking sun-kissed wine in the warm sun, both quite tipsy now, and the young men watched. Soon, their eyes shining with lust as they looked at each other, gauging how drunk the women were before they made their move out there in the deep blue sea, all alone to do what they wanted with these beautiful creatures. Who would care? Certainly no one on shore. It was their boat, their company. They all knew that that these luscious women were starving for real men, and they were just the men to give it to them. None of women who had come before them had ever complained anyhow.

They came to the women, two men, two watching them, waiting their turn. Whoa, whoa, here we go! So damned much fun! Who knew? It would be different this time for the women, not boring at all and they got to the point where they truly did not mind the "assaults" on their bodies. What could they do about it way out here in the middle of the ocean anyway, they asked each other. All day long they took them whenever the mood struck the young healthy young men, studs every one of them. At night they'd stop and drink their rum, the boat drifting in the bright blue sea under the moonlight. The women stayed on deck. Those stars, my God, Danielle, I could stay here forever. They were having the time of their life, that was for sure and why not? McNally was with his whores and evidently Paul was too according to Gloria. Figures Danielle said.

The boys held them hostage, not letting them dive because they were afraid they'd get away from them, but they didn't ask anyway. It was far too nice up here on this happy boat. The men ate some sort of concoction prepared for them by their wives or mothers and the women drank and ate small cakes and sandwiches that they had brought and stored in the little refrigerator, and the men were constantly grilling fish on the little grill in the corner, so there certainly was plenty to eat for all. They men knew that all women loved them and lusted after their over-sized penises. They would catch hell when they got to shore, they also knew too well, but it didn't faze any of them at all. It was worth every second. Their women always came after them, knowing they had rollicked with the customers...even if they hadn't. They didn't care how fat, how old, or how ugly they were. Always acting so innocent, the women would fume. And their lives were hell. They would head back out to the big beautiful blue sea as soon as possible whether there were paying customers or not. They wanted the simple life without all the drama their women brought nonstop. They would come to shore to eat and then buy groceries if they had any money and then head back out to their sapphire blue haven. They could always find fish to cook on the little gas stove. Life just couldn't be better and Mama Josetta always had cake and bread for them before they slipped quietly back out to the freedom of the deep sapphire blue sea that they loved so much.

On their flight home, Gloria began to confide in her friend.

"You know Paul is queer as a two dollar bill, right?"

"What? Are you sure? Did you actually catch him in the act?"

"No, Luke told me. He goes with him on the weekends to play with the hookers and he latched onto the men who came to do a show with the women."

"Is McNally having sex with men too, Gloria?"

"Are you kidding me? The man told me that he didn't hang around with fags and I damn sure better keep that piece of shit away from him."

"I'm so sick of him, sick to death. I don't understand him at all. Our sex life is amazing, I'm not kidding; it's out of this world wonderful, at least to me it is, but it's just not enough for him, Gloria. He takes off every chance he gets to be with other women. I've been thinking about it a lot and I just want it to be over now."

"I'm sorry to hear that Danielle. I know he loves you but some men are just too weak to be involved with just one woman. I myself don't think it's such a bad thing; it actually frees me up to do whatever I want, but I guess I'm an unusual woman, to say the least. To be honest, our sex life has always lacked passion; it has simply been an act of release for Paul and of course the best way we knew to have the family we always wanted. Nothing more. That experience there on the boat was an amazing thing for me. I've never experienced passion like that. I'll be forever grateful for those young men. What fun that was!"

"That's really sad, Gloria. You deserve to know real passion; every woman does. It breaks my heart to think about walking away from Luke, but I just can't do it anymore. There is a limit to my passion and love for that awful man. He'll come see his kids, of course, if he even wants to that is; I wouldn't ever want to keep him away from them, but it's over between us now. I've definitely made up my mind about this."

They flew into Savannah at around 7:00 that evening and went their separate ways. Danielle went to her children and cuddled them and kissed them soundly. Her youngest twins' eyes were open now and they were actually able to focus on her face. So damned cute! They were both still so tiny, especially when compared to bigger boys. So beautiful; the two of them so different from the others. Funny how the boys all looked like

Daddy and her little angel was the spitting image of her, definitely of Mexican descent. She rocked them to sleep and then went to her bedroom and called Luke.

"McNally here." He said. She could hear the music and the voices in the background. A real party there for him and his whores.

"Where you been, Danielle? You're a fucking mother now so why don't you start acting like one."

"Oh, you mean like you? Coming home to your wife and kids every night like a good daddy should?" She spit, wondering how the hell the man even knew she was gone. He certainly never came home.

"Fuck you, why should I have to do everything? I'm a man. It's the woman's job."

"I didn't ask you to do anything. I'm really sorry that your children are such a burden to you that you don't even want to come home. I want a divorce, Luke. You don't have to come home anymore. I'm having the locks changed before you even get your stinking ass out of bed, so don't bother us anymore. You're free now to live your life as you please."

"Don't bother, Danielle. I've already filed the divorce papers at the court house. We'll have a hearing in a couple of weeks if I can push it through quickly. They'll send you a notice in the mail, just be there or don't, it doesn't matter one fucking bit to this man."

And she slammed the phone down. Good, one last thing to worry about, she said out loud as she went to the kitchen and grabbed her bottle of champagne. Charlene came out of her bedroom and she told her that they were getting a divorce.

"Well, I can't say that he'll be missed much around here, that's for sure."

In the morning, she and Charlene packed up everything in the house that belonged to him into boxes and they drove to the office and carried each box to the porch and then drove away. She dropped Charlene off at home and drove to the beach. She walked the surf and then stopped at a restaurant just above the sand and had breakfast before going home to her children. Her fun times were over now and yes, Luke, I will be the boring parent that hadn't been able to hold onto her man for long. She looked forward to being a mother and raising her children alone without the stress of a bad relationship. And she knew there would be fun, just different from the fun she had experienced up to now, lots of happy times as the children grew older.

Luke McNally, Attorney at Law, left his office in the early evening after his last client had left for the day and began to walk; he needed to calm down and think. He had fumed all day. He found the boxes on the porch and the sadness that swept over him almost took him to his knees; but this wasn't working for either of them, he thought, ignoring the fact that he hadn't gone home or that he refused to give up his lovely escorts. When he was calm again, he went back to the office and made out the divorce papers, readying them to be filed first thing in the morning. It's over now thank God, I'm finally free after three long years; even a year was too long with that woman, he thought. But Luke McNally didn't know why he felt that way or why he was so angry that he didn't want to go home anymore. The only thing he knew for certain was that she wanted to smother him and control him and make him stay home and be a good little boy, but he was having none of that.

Danielle had procured the services of a divorce attorney, which set him to fuming once again. The woman was asking for an outrageous amount of money for support for the children and she also had the nerve to ask for alimony. He was going to fight this with everything he had and he was certain he would win.

He set the court date for as soon as possible. The judge was not exactly a friend, but they certainly knew each other. A little too sarcastic for him, but he'd do. He thought about his lovely escorts. He'd call them for tonight, but he didn't. He was just sick to death of women. There was a good strong hand right there at the end of his arms, for God's sake, and it didn't cost him a penny. But he certainly had learned his lesson the hard way that was for sure. Maybe he'd be a fag too. Nah. Same ole boring shit, and AIDs to boot. No, no fucking way! He couldn't stand to watch Paul. It was disgusting! He wouldn't allow the fags or his used to be friend to come to the office again. Damn Fag!!! I've got my work to sustain me and now I'm going to get down to business and start making some serious money again; then, when he had enough, he'd buy a boat and he'd disappear again, this time for good, even though money was simply no issue for the man; he could buy 20 sea going yachts if that's what he wanted.

The thought of getting back to work and eventually buying a boat that he could live on cheered him up tremendously, and he was anxious to just get Danielle and her 5 little bastards gone from his miserable life for good. It was time to be happy again before it was too late. He certainly wasn't getting any younger. He was moving on toward 40 years old now and he felt the clock ticking away slowly; too young to feel so old, so worn out, but there it was; just the way his life's path was destined to travel, he thought morosely, feeling terribly sorry for himself; but this too would pass and he'd be back to this old self again, a smarter man then he had been.

Three months later, it was time to go to court. She knew where he was, she knew today was the day. She had received the papers from the courts and she had planned to be there. She talked to her lawyer and told him that she would like for him to represent her in court to which he agreed. When the time came, she just couldn't force herself to sit in the courtroom and listen to what McNally had to say about her. This was going to be a cut and dry case and he'd be in and out of the courtroom in no time at all, her attorney told her. All three of the women thought that they'd go, but the babies were sleeping on the warm grass under a big umbrella and the other toddlers were busy with plastic buckets and little shovels, digging happily in their sand box. Gloria's boys were at tennis lessons or archery or some such shit. And the day was gorgeous and the iced white wine with fruit flowed. Too fine a day to spend inside listening to his bullshit, Danielle said. There was no good reason for that anymore. It was late autumn and Thanksgiving was right around the corner. They would make a meal with all the side dishes and invite everyone they could think of, they said as Birdie, Charlene's nickname, made a list. They would have to move quickly if they wanted to give everyone time to RSVP the dinner or not, giving them plenty of time to decide one way or another. Maybe Paul and his new lover would come, and he could finally introduce him to his boys now. That might be fun. Then winter would come and it would be time to stay indoors then, lying around in front of the fireplace, watching old movies and listening to long forgotten records. The old fashioned ones, the love songs from long ago that Danielle loved so much.

"Can you still have children, Charlene, or are you in menopause yet?" Gloria asked Birdie.

"What the hell? I'm only 33 fucking years old. What the hell? It's these fat cheeks and these awful flabby arms, bye-bye arms my mother calls them. My legs look like a damned bird which is where I got that ridiculous nickname! Not a damned thing I can do about it. I was born like this; my whole family actually is not very attractive. It's just not in our genes." She said as flipped her arms and the skin swayed back and forth as it hung there to show them how ugly she was.

"Not one man ever has shown me an ounce of interest, not ever! I absolutely hate my body! And all my stinking ancestors too. It just isn't fair!" She lamented to her surprised friends.

"Hey, hey, don't give up?" Danielle said. "I'd say it's time for some more plastic surgery, my friend. It solves so many feminine woos. You deserve a big strong Marine too!" Something Gloria had talked about, wondering how she would ever meet an officer in the Marine Corp or if it was even possible.

"Yeah, right. If only." She said sadly, looking out at the forest of trees in the distance. "I'll never have that kind of money, not ever."

"Bullshit! McNally owes you everything after what you've had to put up with from that rich asshole. He's just going to have to let some of that go. It's for a good cause. He doesn't have a clue what's there anyway. I keep track very closely, at least I used to. Too much now to even bother counting anymore. I swear, it's just too boring for words. And the stupid ass couldn't close the accounts or keep me out thanks to my lawyer, but we need to do it ASAP just in case the judge allows him to do that. He'll move his money, but even if he does,

I've got my own accounts and I'm worth a whole lot of money too."

Gloria hit send and made an appointment, first with the plastic surgeon. The woman didn't need hair; she had more than a human being needed, but the dentist was next. Then they talked about Camp Lejeune. Danielle wasn't allowed; they'd never be able to meet anyone if she was there. Geez! Some friends you are. Too bad, so sad Lady. You're going to have to find your own man all on your own. You're just going to have to suck it up and lay in that bed you made for yourself for now, Gloria teased her.

"Thanks loads, girlfriends. You're not allowed in my house or my pool ever again, you know."

Fine with me, they said. Well fuck you all then. And they drank their wine, quite drunk again. Are we winos? Yep, of course we are, they said happily. Let's swim naked. Let's go! And the babies played happily in the sand that was all over their little chubby faces. Yummy!!

There was no reason of course for Birdie to leave town to have her plastic surgery and Danielle followed Gloria's advice for the excellent plastic surgeon she felt would do a bang up job on their friend. It would take time because she wouldn't bc able to have everything done at the same time which would be too many unnecessary hours under anesthesia; however, that was fine with Birdie. She was a patient woman and would be glad to wait it out.

"I wonder how the hearing is going. When he hears what he has to pay, he'll just walk out. If he isn't back by the time Charlene is better, we'll just drop the babies at the office for the weekend." She told the girls, which is exactly what they ended up having to do.

When they drove up, he was standing at the porch, leaning on the railing and smoking a cigar.

"Oh SHIT!! Birdie, help me."

He flipped, chasing her down as they carried the babies into the office and dragging her back to the car by her hair; he tried to force a child into her arms, and when she wouldn't take the child, he carried them one at a time out to the car and just tossed them in the back seat like sacks of potatoes.

"You all drive safely, you stupid fucking winos, ya all hear?" He said, grinning down at Gloria through the window.

"Hey woman! What the fuck did you do to yourself? You might look a tad better, if I don't say so myself, but it ain't gonna do you a damn bit of good, Doc. The man you ain't been fucking has finally had to turn to all those sweet little boys just to get a little relief for his queer dick, so…..dream on sweet thing. He need's assholes, but just not yours cause you ain't it, Lady." He said conversationally, leaning in the window in her face. But she kept him busy, telling him about her trip to New York, blah, blah, blah, but he lost interest almost immediately and turned away as she talked.

Shut the fuck up, he said as he walked back to the office.

Stupid women. Just spending our money. Worthless!

Danielle and Charlene had quietly taken the babies back out of the car and took them quickly back to the office at a silent run while Gloria kept him busy. They sat the toddlers in the reception room quickly and laid the babies on the floor in their infant seats, leaving plenty of bottles and diapers, and pullups and then they slipped quietly back into the car before Luke was aware of their deceit. Gloria immediately started the car and drove out of the small parking lot as they laughed and high 5-ed each other. When he realized what they had done, he ran after them, pounding on the trunk until Gloria hit the gas and he almost fell to the ground, screaming BITCHES at the top of his lungs. I'll kill you, you fucking cunts!! He shouted to the road as they disappeared from sight.

The minute I can, I'll slip back into the house and I'll slit her throat and bury her in the back yard, and then the fucking fat nanny. If Gloria comes nosing around, I'll slit her throat and put her with the others; plenty of land back there in that fucking forest and the shovel's in the shed. No, I'll rent a tractor! And he went inside to his children. That bitch was gone again for heaven knew how long. He called the supermarket and had baby food and cookies and milk delivered; everything he thought they would need to keep them until she came to get them. He settled in to be with the children for however long he had with them.

She waited until Sunday, but he didn't bring the babies back home. He must be waiting for her to come and get them, such a lazy ass, she thought as she got into the SUV and drove to the office. When she drove up close to the door, he came out onto the porch and leaned on the railing, watching her. She sat in the car, trying to gauge whether or not he had something planned for her. God, he was so gorgeous, she thought as she looked at him, grinning his sexy, lazy grin as he watched her. She got out and walked into the office, ignoring him now. They didn't say a word to each and he sure as hell didn't help put the children into the car either. No wonder she hated him so much. He was such a loser. She got them belted in and then drove off, not looking back as she drove out onto the street, and then she began to cry softly. Her heart was breaking. What was it about that cruel, nasty man that could take her to her knees, even when he treated her like she was dirt? He broke her heart, never having a clue or caring if she was hurting or not.

Court was a joke.

"Your Honor, please, just listen to me for a minute, John, you just aren't being fair! I'm telling you the truth; those damned kids aren't even mine. It hurts me to say this but the bitch is a fucking slut." He said clearly, his words bouncing loudly into the courtroom, making everyone sit up straighter. Now we're talking!!

Of course the judge knew he was lying, but he sure as hell had to try.

"And to make matters even worse, your Honor, she's just about spent every cent I have. There's nothing left to even feed her little bastards, your Honor, and I sure don't have the finances anymore. The stupid Mexican whore is going to have go on welfare, just no other way around it Judge."

John sighed. Here we go.

"Mr. McNally, true or not, she's the woman you married till death do you part and 5 innocent children were born during that union.

"I'm going to slit her throat as soon as I can get my babies adopted out to someone responsible and decent." He spurted out, so frustrated he wanted to kick someone. The bitch couldn't win here, she just couldn't!

"I thought you just said they weren't yours." He said, the court room exploding in laughter. "You are hereby ordered to pay $10,000 a month alimony and $1500 per child."

"Your HONOR!! There are 5 kids who aren't even mine!!" But John just pounded his gavel and asked for the next person to come forward. "You Rotten Bastard!" He yelled at the cold-hearted man.

"That's another $10,000 to be paid immediately." John said as the court room rolled. "Bailiff, take him down to the treasury office right now. If you say another word Mr. McNally you will be spending some well-deserved time in jail and what you'll pay will be nothing compared to what you're going to pay each month."

He kept his mouth shut and walked out of the court, moving to the door quickly to make his getaway, heading to the big doors at the end of the hallway and outside to freedom. He would fight this and if he couldn't, well, tough shit; they were just going to have accept small monthly payments. But the bailiff grabbed his arm and escorted him somewhere where he was forced to cough up the money or go to jail, and a uniformed cop followed behind them to make certain he didn't bolt. Son-of-a-bitch!

The next day, he ordered a small, bright red tractor to be delivered to the house. He was so proud of that thing when it finally came, looking at his shiny baby all day long. He was ready. The bitch had seen her last moments on earth. Where was she anyway? She hadn't been in court and he hadn't heard a single word from her for a while. He wondered if she was even home or if she took off on some sort of adventure again.

She was on birth control this time and she had had a steel door made to look like wood put up to keep him out of his bedroom just in case he came home and started his shit again. She knew the man was coming home. Court had been a disaster and she got a blow by blow account of the hearing from an old friend who had been there and witnessed the hilarious performance first hand. They both laughed so hard, her belly hurt.

She had a man come put in the metal door that looked just like wood to match all the other doors in the house and then install a sliding metal bolt. He had to be curious, but he simply smiled as he worked. Women; can't live with them, can't live without them. Someone knew exactly what they were talking about, that was for sure.

There. Locked tight against his ugly cheating ass, she said as she shoved the bolt into the metal clasp. She made coffee, took some Advil for the headache that was just beginning to pound and read for the rest of the day as the babies cried and played and pooped and ate. New York City wore her out, but that was stupid, it had been months ago.

And here came Luke McNally, Attorney at Law.

"Where's the nanny?"

"You fired her, remember?" She lied. He was too dumb to know one way or another if this was true or not and this was just down right fun.

"You call her this minute and tell her to get her fat ugly ass back here now! I'm still paying that lousy cunt!"

"You call her, you fired her." She lied, trying to hide her laughter as she sipped her hot coffee.

He hit send on his phone and the minute she picked up, he lit into her.

"You get here right now, do you hear me? Yes it's McNally! Who else would it be? I'm the one you fuck every chance you get. You owe me money ugly lady.

Do you hear me? I've been paying you for months and you just took off like it was free money! Talk about taking advantage. I'll sue your fat ass. Get here now, Goddamnit!" He said and slammed his phone shut.

"Oh, that ought to bring her running, you fool."

"My God, look at you, Birdie. You look like an angel!" She said, just amazed at the transformation as she walked through the door.

"I can't quit looking in the mirror. I cried for the first two days."

"I know you did, I was there remember? Your mother and sister cried too. That was a trip to remember. So shocked! Mr. Marine, here you come."

"Shit no!"

"What the hell? All that work done for nothing then!"

"Not for nothing. For me, Danielle! But I certainly have no intentions of ever, ever leaving this hilarious, loud, stupid house. This is where my laughter lives." She said as she leaned against the dresser.

McNally watched them from his perch on the bed. He had followed them in there to stop them from spending any more money. Didn't the stupid woman realize that he was broke now?

"Good. I'm going to need you more than ever very soon. I want to open an office and start a practice as soon as the babies get just a little older. I'm certainly not getting any younger, that's for sure."

"Yeah, that's for damned sure, Lady." He said from his perch.

""Shut the hell up, McNally."

He stayed on the bed and listened until he became quite alarmed.

"Shit, knock it off you two useless....You buy one thing, one more fucking thing, you stupid sluts and you're dead by morning!" He threatened from his perch on the bed, serious as could be once again. But the soon to be bright red tractor would be sitting in the shed, happily waiting. He'd kill both of the useless whores.

They laughed, and they shopped.

"Peach for you I think. It will set off your blue eyes and then some pinkish orange lipstick. Let's get eyelashes. Not the magnetic ones, they're useless. They fall off whenever you blink."

"Why would you wear eyelashes?"

"Well I never have, but it might be fun. We'll cut them and glue them to our own eyelashes, or better yet, we'll get a beautician to do it."

"Aw, shit, stupid fucking cunts" he said from his perch, totally interested in what women did and what they talked about. "Stupid sluts." He mumbled as he listened to them.

"Will you have lovers, do you think, Birdie?"

"Of course! I still have that apartment. We'll go there."

"You better believe that one, Sister. Highly unlikely anyone will want to do anything indecent to a big assed woman, though. You're just too damned ugly, Lady." Drinking whiskey now, a cigar lit, stinking up the bedroom, still listening to the crazy whores.

"I've never gotten to moan with passion, Danielle. I want to feel that. I want to be talked to by some big good-looking man who will slip into the shower with me, talking lovely filth; I want to wake up with a man riding me like stupid does." She said, leaning her elbows on the dresser close to her friend who sat at the computer

AWWWW, shit! Was nothing sacred anymore? He tried to ignore them, but unlike his lazy Mexican wife, he just couldn't. He got up and went to his children; he pulled the toddlers from the cribs and fed the brats. He pulled the tiny females and sat them on the rug. His two fat boys were getting so big now but like Morgan, they'd lose all that baby fat now that they were walking around more, but it made him sad because he loved their fat roly-poly bodies. Someone made breakfast, catering to the lazy woman who was exhausted from spending his hard earned money. Two peas in a pod he thought. He was going to fire the nanny before the week was out. He had to do all the work anyway, he thought, totally disgusted as he pulled two Pull-Ups...it never ends, God.

"When is it my turn?" He said quite loudly to the ceiling. Gloria, Birdie and Danielle laughed and drank coffee as they listened to his whining call to God.

"The man says this is my last week again."

"Yeah, I heard. Hey, do you want to learn to learn to scuba dive and take off with me and Gloria? We can't go far now, but there's plenty to see in the waters around here."

"What's that? You mean like put on a tank with air and go into the ocean where there are vicious sharks just waiting to attack?" She asked.

He pulled off the brats diapers. He wished to all that was holy that his bride had disappeared for good this time. It just never ended, he thought, so weary he wanted to hide.

"That's it God. No more friendly talks ever again. I've had it with you. Don't ever come around here again, you stupid ugly jerk. You're just about as useless as they come! And you're useless son and mother too. No good for anyone if you ask me!"

He followed his wife around the house, wearing her out as she drank and got drunk. It's not even noon lady! You'll never be anything else but a wino, that's for damned sure, he assured her, drinking his whiskey straight from the bottle and smoking his beloved cigar. A phallus she called it. Shit!

"It's after 5 o'clock half-wit." She said, not in the mood to put up with his endless games again.

Time sure flew when you were having fun, he thought, as he drank and smoked, filled to the brim with sexual energy. He threw her book against the far wall and she just left it there, smoking, drinking, the same old nastiness floating around her head softly. Idiot. And this was why the alcohol, the incessant need for that wine to numb her brain. She got up and went to the bed, slamming the bolt home before she got into the shower. He came to the door hearing the shower. Perfect. He'd hide and wait. Nothing better than sex with a nice clean vagina, that's for damned sure! But he couldn't budge the door. It didn't take him long to realize that it was made of steel and he finally gave up. What a lousy evil Mexican whore; heartless, just heartless.

He went back to the couch with his liquor and cigar and good ole TV. The older football games were back on now. He finally lay back on the couch and was snoring loudly within minutes. Oh thank God. A reprieve. She thought about stabbing him in the heart as he slept. She'd never get caught she knew. She could drive a bright red tractor too.

The next morning he went to the Home Depot and bought a nice wooden and very hollow door, matching it as closely as he could to the color there now. He talked to the man and was shown the hardware and the tools needed to take the old one down and put up the new one with a knob that didn't have a lock. He put it in the back of his SUV which had dark windows all around, locked the doors tight, and then went inside to the quiet house and called Gloria. They talked for a few minutes as she wondered what on earth he was calling her for. He hadn't done that in in a very long time, ever since he and Paul had parted ways.

"Hey, I've been thinking. Both Danielle and Charlene have been stuck here in this house for a while now. Neither one has been able to get out and just have a fun day, you know? I was thinking that maybe you could come over and invite them to lunch and then talk them into going shopping or something. What do you think?"

She was quite surprised to say the least, but she hadn't spent time out in the city with her friends in a very long time and she needed to just get out and enjoy the day too. She agreed and they hung up from each other and he waited.

The minute they drove off, he carried the door into the house and set to work. He had zero experience so he knew it was going to take a couple of hours at least, but it didn't. He had all the necessary tools and was given step by step instructions from one of the men that worked in hardware. He was finished in less than hour. First taking down the old, quite heavy door and putting up the much lighter one, and then cutting a round hole for the door knob. He left the door open so that she wouldn't notice anything suspicious, and then he carried the very heavy door out to the SUV and drove it his shed and locked it in. There now. She was his. He'd be really nice, he planned, talking pleasantly, getting her champagne....again and again until she was good and drunk but not close to being unconscious unless it was absolutely necessary, and then when she went to bed, he'd pounce as only a real man can pounce. Ideally, he wanted his bride completely awake. And he was going to make her groan all night long, he planned.

He finally got her, waking her to his fat disgusting tongue, confused, so tired, too much damned champagne. She wouldn't respond; she couldn't. But of course she did, grabbing his hair and writhing, her little hips bouncing. Then he mounted and rammed, his arm in the air bronco riding style. EEE-HAAA! RIDE UM COWBOY. Stupid half-wit! But then she gave him her little scream. She deliberately scratched his back with her long bright red nails, but he didn't feel it, not now anyway. In the morning, she'd pour rubbing alcohol on the wounds when he came to her whining about the pain just to hear him scream. It was the least she could do.

He'd have his fun and slit both women's throats in the early morning hours. He had to get rid of the woman and no amount of amazing sex was going to change one damn thing. It was just time. Tomorrow was going to be a busy day for him because his lovely red tractor was finally being delivered. Let the good times roll!! He was snoring within minutes. Such a boring asshole, she thought, listening to the racket coming from the sleeping man. A real man never changed his manly routine, he'd tell her; whatever the hell that meant.

And he'd been so nice and concerned for his little darling that Gloria might even testify on his behalf, but for now, he had to get her to sign papers to release him from his financial obligations now that he had stopped the divorce before the 3-month waiting period was up. He simply did not want there to be any doubt when she disappeared, and her releasing him from this obligation would make it seem that they were a happy couple again. He was home and they were living in seeming harmony, happy with each other at last, at least until she disappeared one day, just walking out the door and leaving him with the children. He remembered his threat to the judge about murdering her, but that was just hearsay and he'd get out of that one in a New York second. No proof whatsoever. He'd tell people that his wife was so unhappy, just tired of being a mother and wife to such a boring dedicated man, and so she just walked out on him and the children. Yeah, that would work.

He went to his office and made out the financial resolution form, stating that he was back home and all was well, releasing him from the almost $20,000 a month payment. He'd have to wait for a while to kill her, not even thinking about how exactly he planned to execute the deed, only seeing the beautiful grave site way out there, far, far from his happy home.

He brought the papers back and asked her to sit at the kitchen table so that they could talk, which she did, really curious. He handed her the papers and laid a pen on the table so that she could sign. She sat quietly, reading everything, and then got up and carried them back to the office with him following, starting to get anxious now.

She moved close to the shredder, pretending to still read the legal paper as he kept thrusting the pen at her, but the lousy fucking Mexican whore slut wasn't cooperating. Then she flipped on the shredder and before he could stop her it was gone.

"Sorry. I don't agree with any of this."

"Are you serious? How are you going to feed all those bastards you gave birth to if I take my money and disappear, and I will, believe me, I will!!"

Okay, here we go again. My bastards, he said, obviously born illegitimately and he certainly wasn't the father of course.

"Sorry. I need to talk to an attorney before signing anything."

"But I'm a fucking attorney, you stupid Mexican whore!" He shouted in frustration. What the hell!!

She simply brushed past him and then began to laugh hysterically, holding her stomach as she hung onto the desk. She knew exactly what he was up to.

OH MY GOD! He thought, watching her and feeling desperation wash over him. If she didn't sign this, there was no fucking way he'd get away with her murder. No one in his right mind would believe a fucking word he said. OH MY GOD! Okay, okay, calm down and think. Time to buy a boat and just get my ass out of this hell-hole, he finally concluded, storming out of the office and getting into his SUV. He'd close all of his accounts and just take his money with him. There was no way she'd ever see a penny. Let's see how she likes that one.

When he got the call that his little red tractor was on its way to the house, he hopped into the car and drove back to the house to wait, so excited. He ran out and talked to the man who showed him how to start it and back it up. He took it to the good sized shed he'd had installed as soon as he got back home. The grave digger needed a good home after all. It was small and red with a big shovel in the front and the cab was enclosed in glass so that he could dig even when it was cold, but of course, that just wouldn't work for him, the ground would be too hard and impossible to dig up until it warmed up again, so he sure better get busy and find the grave site now, he thought, while the weather was still warm. He played with it all day, riding around, looking, and looking until he found the perfect spot at the far end of his property. He had 10 acres backed by a nice dark forest, so perfect for his plans. He drove a little ways into the thick trees and there it was. Absolutely the most perfect place ever. When he covered the graves, he'd plant wild flowers and some grass to cover any evidence that the earth had been disturbed. Perfect, perfect, perfect!! Plenty of room for two if it came to that. He parked the tractor, locking it in with a big padlock and then he walked back to the house. And there she was, standing in the road, watching him with an evil smile on her face. He simply brushed past her, totally ignoring the smirking woman.

It didn't take her long to figure out what McNally was up to. He was looking for grave sites. He had told her often enough that he was going to kill her and bury her out there where no one would find the body. She watched and she laughed. This man was a fucking hoot. He really planned to do this and she loved the thought. He was so stupid; he wouldn't even know how to begin; the man didn't even own a gun, for God's sake. He must be planning to strangle her; what else could it be? But she sure as hell had her gun close by and she certainly knew how to use it, but of course, she knew instinctively that it would never come to that. She turned, walking beside him and began to talk idly, just making conversation. He was trying to ignore her, not listening at all.

"Hey, McNally." She said, looping her arm though his. "Did I ever tell you that my father owned a big construction company? When I got into junior high school, he would take me to the site and he taught me how to drive that big machine. It was nothing like that puny thing out there. Oh no. It was huge. He would let me dig the holes to start the foundations, and I have to tell you, I was quite good at it. It was something I loved to do. I could dig holes all day long. Did I ever tell you that, Honey?"

What? What the fuck! his mind shouted, alarm bells screaming. This wasn't right! What was she saying? OH MY GOD! This woman was planning his death; he just knew it. What had he ever done to her to deserve such a horrible fate? He knew her and he knew she'd do it too. He would have to watch the bitch like a hawk and if she even looked at him cross-eyed, he'd call the cops and have her arrested in a New York second! He probably better get his ass out of here and get back to the office, but no, she had the key and he knew she would hide it from him and come in the night as he slept. She had a gun and she also had a knife. He'd find them immediately, he thought, walking fast now as she slowed and walked behind him, laughing so evilly, scaring him half to death. What the hell was he going to do? He had no way to fight off a vicious Mexican; he surely knew that he would be hard pressed to protect himself once she set her sights on him, and he was afraid.

He went into the house and poured a very large glass of his fine whiskey to calm himself. He lit a cigar and sat on the couch, waiting and watching her every movement, planning his escape. He thought again about the big boat he was going to buy. He couldn't put it off any longer. Lousy cunt, but of course he didn't say it out loud. He'd be real nice from now on until he could kill the fucking bitch in her sleep, he thought, calming down now.

When she went into the kitchen to start preparing dinner, he got up and quietly went into the bedroom, looking for the gun. He opened every drawer and put his big hand in, feeling for anything cold and metal.

"Hey, McNally, Focus!! The gun's in the closet."

He hadn't expected her to be standing there in the doorway and he visibly jumped out of his skin, his bowels turning to water as he tried desperately not to shit his pants, clenching his butt cheeks tight. When he felt in control of his bowels again, he pulled the closet door open and there it was. Good, he'd keep an eye on it and as soon as she fell asleep, he'd hide all the bullets so that there was nothing to shoot with.

And then she moved out of the doorway and went back to the kitchen. He walked over to the pillows and lifted each one, looking for the Mexican's knife. That was really what scared him more than anything. Mexicans liked to gut people, adding that extra twist just for fun.

"The knife is in the kitchen drawer, Honey."

Again he jumped, trying desperately trying not to shit his pants for sure this time as his bowels turned to water. And she laughed, getting a big kick out of his obvious surprise and fear. Sneaky, evil little Mexican slut. He just couldn't help it. He was scared, goddamnit!

The woman was evil personified with those cold black eyes always looking at him, watching him, he thought as he remembered the walk down the path to the house earlier today. And still she laughed. The woman laughed way too much lately as far as he was concerned. She must be slowly going insane and he was in real danger here, he thought as he snuck quietly to the living room couch where his liquor and cigar sat waiting for him. Then he turned on football and forgot all about it. It was going to be a good game for sure this time.

And then she called Gloria. She curled up at the other end of the couch and began to tell her about the tractor and how he was going to kill her if he could, but of course, he would never be able to....on and on, really pissing him off!! They laughed at him, getting a big kick at his expense. He'd have to kill that rotten bitch too he thought. And lucky for him, the stupid woman was always hanging around his home, drinking his liquor and eating his food; it wouldn't be a problem at all. No sireee. Three birds with one stone. Hey, officer, they all three took off to someplace far away. One was fat and ugly as sin with no hope for any kind of future and one was tired of her adoring husband and darling little children and the other was married to a fucking fag who wasn't interested in her old worn out pussy anymore. Yeah, the judge would fall for that one for sure.

He looked down at all the babies. All his boys had big hands and big feet. Ugly little fuckers, he said out loud. But the penises, now that was a different story. Just like your Daddy, he said. Gonna be big enough to make all the ladies sing with joy. Gonna be just like your old man, he told them again, and then he had to swallow hard to push back the tears sliding down his cheeks unchecked as joy filled his veins, flooding his soul with the happiness he could no longer contain. Boy's God! Boys! And these beautiful baby girls, so delicate and lovely with their curly black hair and big eyes. There were babies everywhere! He wondered if they would have more; he sure hoped so. There was certainly plenty of room for more....well maybe not, but there was plenty of space to add more rooms, that was for damned sure, obviously forgetting all about his vow to kill his wife in the very near future.

He picked them up and kissed them one at a time and then diapered those that needed it. Time to poddy train the two middle guys now. Just watch daddy's wee-wee, he told the boys as they fought and screamed over one thing or another, not the least bit interested in what their daddy was doing with his wee-wee. One bit, one pulled hair. They got that from the Mexican lying on the couch, probably drunk already by now. He sat in the rocker, just watching them as they played and fought. His oldest played with a big police car and then his fire truck quietly, not paying attention to anything around him, lost in his own little imagination.

With time he went into Morgan and Devon's room and put them down for their afternoon nap and then little Gabriella and Savanna. Michael seldom cooperated any more now that he was 3; evidently naps just weren't for him anymore. He would be starting preschool in another year. Can you believe it? They just grow up too fast. And then there were his little girls, so incredibly lovely. Just like the Mexican lying on her ass on the couch. They were 5 months already and just cute as could be. The time was going by just too fast. The boys played quietly with their endless supply of toys, plastic and furry alike, while the youngest ones sucked pacifiers. He was so happy. He'd feed them when they woke up, of course. No one else in this house ever cooked or got off their lazy asses. He'd fire Birdie first thing in the morning, he swore. He had rocked the babies and talked to his sons, laying the tiny ones on the big rug as he listened to Morgan tell Devon all about it.

He could see the Christmas tree. Danielle had gone all out for the holidays this year and had hired a crew to decorate the house and the lawn. He could hear Christmas carols singing as the elves worked. There would be plenty of toys for every child this year if they behaved. This was going to be the best Christmas he had ever, ever had. And his eyes began to glisten as liquid welled up and fell down his cheeks once again, tears of joy streaking down his stubble-bound chin. You never shave! Danielle always yelled at him. Just for you, my little slut.

Thank you my Father, Thank you my precious Jesus and Mary. You've heaped blessing on the shoulders of this old man, who certainly never did a damn thing to deserve all of this. Amen. Merry Christmas to all, the angels sang above him, their beautiful wings spread wide.

He thought about Christmas and what he would buy for his sweet wife and their hard working nanny, just a blessing to the family, he thought kindly. They both worked so hard. It couldn't be easy, but they never complained. He wanted to buy them each a wonderful gift this year, and money would be no issue for them, feeling so generous this Christmas. He wondered what they would like, but he didn't have a clue. He had never asked the stupid broads what they wanted anyway, suddenly flipping back to anger and disgust. They stole his money every chance they got. He had never even thought about a gift, not even for Danielle's birthday; the bitch just didn't deserve anything as far as he was concerned, thought Luke McNally, Attorney at Law as he did a complete turn-around, becoming his typical nasty-assed self once again. Mr. McMizer McNally the evil Mexican woman called him. Yeah, I wonder why, Bitch!

And besides that, the "man" was out there just waiting for him to walk through their doors so that they could gouge him, greedy fuckers! Probably of Jewish descent, every fucking one of them. He had no personal experience with Jews, at least as far as he knew, but he had heard the rumors. Well, he was certainly having none of that that was for damn sure. He wasn't born yesterday after all. So he scrapped the idea of gifts before it could become a reality. Stupid fucking bitches, lying around on their asses all day, getting drunk, spending his money, and the cunts never lifted a finger in the house anymore, even though he never had either, but somehow the house always sparkled. Shit no, not now, not ever! They deserved nothing as far as he was concerned.

He had heard Gloria telling the women just this morning that he definitely needed to talk to a psychiatrist and maybe get on some sort of psycho pills. She told them that he could actually be dangerous if he didn't get some help fast. And then the dumb bitch left a card with some idiot's name on it, another damned woman of course. Like she would have a clue as to what men have to endure just to keep his goddamned family together and happy! Ha, not hardly! So, too bad, so sad, Gloria wasn't getting anything for Christmas either. He was no fool, Mr. McMiser McNally said out loud to no one in particular.

He sat there for a while, just watching the boys. Thank you my Father, thank you my precious Jesus and your mother too, Jesus. You've heaped so many blessings on the shoulders of this old man, he said again. Amen.

And Merry Christmas to all, the angels sang from every corner of the room, their beautiful wings spread wide as they slowly drifted along the ceiling looking down on the little family. Joy to the World and all the creatures on the face the earth. It's Christmas and the Christ Child has come. Halleluiah, Halleluiah. It's Christmas.

Printed in the United States
by Baker & Taylor Publisher Services